THE GRACIE STORIES
LEAH CUTTER

Knotted Road Press
www.KnottedRoadPress.com

THE GRACIE STORIES
LEAH CUTTER

ALSO BY LEAH CUTTER

Historic Fantasy:
A Sword's Poem
Paper Mage
The Caves of Buda
The Jaguar and the Wolf

Contemporary Fantasy:
Of Myst and Folly
Poisoned Pearls
The Popcorn Thief
Siren's Call
When the Moon Over Kualina Mountain Comes
Zydeco Queen and the Creole Fairy Courts

The Shadow Wars Trilogy:
The Raven and the Dancing Tiger
The Guardian Hound

The Clockwork Fairy Kingdom Trilogy:
The Clockwork Fairy Kingdom
The Maker, the Teacher, and the Monster

TABLE OF CONTENTS

DEDICATION

To my own (unindicted) co-conspirator.

I couldn't do this without you.

This is Gracie's origin story. It wasn't the first one that I wrote. However, after I wrote the first story, this story just unfolded in my head. It was easy to write—Gracie's voice was very loud in my head. As was Mama, who wanted to see better for her girl, but just didn't know how to get there.

GRACIE AND THE WHIRLIGIG

I don't know where Mama got that damned whirligig. She must've either traded some of her top grade moonshine for it, or she tricked someone out of it. Or maybe a little of both.

When the stupid thing stopped whirring, it looked like a big brass dragonfly, with four wings and a pieced together tail, about the length of my arm. It was damn ugly, with cold metal eyes that bulged out of the side of its head and pinchers at the ends of each of its six twig-thin arms.

When it was whirling, though, I couldn't take aim on it quick enough to shoot it solidly. I don't know why Mama thought I could, but she kept insisting that I try that afternoon, sweating in that open field. The leaves was changing, and the few that still clung to the trees was pretty enough, but hard rains had knocked most of them down.

Gray sky and broiling clouds rolled above me, waiting to pounce and pour down more rain.

Now, I wasn't a bad shot, even for a woman. I could knock a possum out of a tree, single shot straight through the eye. Hell, even at a hundred yards I could still hit a green-and-white-striped winter squash stuck up on a wooden fence post, scatter the guts all over the browning weeds and grass below.

But that damned whirligig was too fast and unpredictable. I couldn't lead it—when I tried, it would scurry some other way I weren't expecting. I hated it with a passion I usually only had for bootleggers who thought they could cheat on what they owed us for our moonshine, falsely believing I couldn't keep the accounts in my head and add up numbers damn quick.

"Again, Gracie," Mama said, her voice grating on me like a wire brush against a sieve.

"Damn it, Mama!" I swore, loading up the old fashioned, black-powder shotgun with more pebbles. She wouldn't let me use the Winchester, or real bullets either, while we was practicing shooting the whirligig. Didn't want me to damage the thing.

I couldn't wait for her to go out on a supply run and leave the whirligig behind. Then we'd see what kind of damage I could do.

I shouldered my shotgun and waited for the buzzing. At least it weren't silent. That would have been too odd. Mama had told me to follow the sound, more than once, but that hadn't ever done me no good.

I had to at least nick the thing. And soon. We didn't have anything for the pot that night, and my traps was empty. And the longer this shooting lesson took, the shorter the afternoon light got, and the chances of us going hungry tonight increased.

To be fair, though, part of my failure was my own fault. I'd been thinking about something other than shooting, thinking about Karly and his brothers, the still his family was running. The bootleggers they was working with, making bigger runs of their moonshine into towns farther away than Hortonsville, maybe even down the rail line to Harrisburg.

The deal they'd been wanting to cut with me.

The bootleggers hated dealing with Mama, but our moonshine was better, so they had to. They all called her crazy, touched, and made signs to ward off evil around her.

Hell, even I'd admit that sometimes Mama weren't all there.

We both knew though, that an unsettled buyer made mistakes, over-ordering and over-paying.

It would've been easier for the bootleggers to deal with me. But I couldn't just cut Mama out. She was family, and that had to count for something. She was my only family too: No brothers or sisters, no cousins who lived close, and no Papa either.

Mama had never been clear about whether she'd run him off or if he'd just run off.

The result was the same: just the pair of us up here in the hills of the Blue Ridge mountains, running the still, selling moonshine to the bootleggers, and making medicinal teas and herbed liquors for the ladies in town. It weren't much of a living, but it was something, at least. I wished for better, but I didn't know what.

Blam.

"What the hell was that?" I asked, lowering my shotgun. I hadn't taken a shot yet.

"Still," Mama said after a moment, then she went running off, the damn whirligig following her like a trained hound, which was always kind of creepy.

Shit. I went running after her, as fast as I could, in the stupid long skirt that Mama insisted that I wear now instead of the pantaloons I'd had as a kid. At least she didn't make me wear a corset or something, not like we could have afforded it.

Stupid Karly and his brothers hadn't decided to take matters into their own hands, had they?

But that was exactly what they'd decided to do. Flames leapt high above the barn the held not only the still and the equipment, but was our only accommodations out here, two rooms in the back and a kitchen to the side. It was brighter than even the Mayor's house in town at Christmas time, with every window lit up with candles.

Mama hadn't paused none but had raced inside, wrapping her hands in her skirt and dragging out what she could save. I followed her. The smoke choked me, and it was like Hell inside, only worse, because it was our still, our dried herbs, our livelihood, our home, that was burning.

I grabbed the first thing I reached, the edge of a table, and started pulling it out. I was blind in that smoke, the flames cackling at me like living things, hungering for my skin.

I don't remember how many times I went into that hellish heat. I dragged out at least one bag of malt and three herb racks. I even rescued the thump keg, though someone had taken an ax to it.

I do remember how choked my breath was, how my lungs felt like they was blocked, how even in the clear air I couldn't breathe without wheezing.

Mama was worse. I finally had to drag her away. She fought me, but she'd also raised me to be as stubborn as she was, so I got her outside and I kept her there. She might have died in that fire.

And maybe that would have been a kinder fate for her.

Instead, we huddled together, shivering in the cold while the rest of what we owned went up in flames. At least the old pines just behind the barn didn't burn. They was far enough away, and the fall had been wet enough that nothing else caught fire.

We coughed like the old miners in town, spitting out black gunk.

The fire might have been pretty against the growing dark, a cheerful light in the blackening woods. But it was turning everything we'd owned to ash.

And I still didn't have any meat for the pot that night either.

☆

The night was long, hard, cold, and wet. We finally both collapsed next to the wrecked barn, too tired to keep moving, keep cleaning, keep accounting for things.

Morning light didn't bring no comfort. We was cold, coughing, out of life and out of luck. We both looked a mess. We share the same pale skin that was even more pale that morning. Our skirts and shirtwaists were sodden and filthy. I had my hair pulled back as tight as I could, but it was black and coarse and useless, mostly. The skin under Mama's eyes—which were dark as the coal they dug up out of the nearby hills—looked bruised.

I'm sure I looked no better. Karly had once told me that my eyes was greener than an elm tree in the spring. It wasn't until two months later that I'd figured out he'd been trying to sweet talk me. I'd just laughed at him at the time.

Had he been planning on setting fire to us ever since?

I scrounged us up some tea, lighter stuff, made from dried dandelion leaves and fragrant root, to help clear our lungs. I restarted the fire outside, where we'd cook together the more fragrant concoctions, as much to get warm as anything else.

The kettle was blackened and battered, but it had been that way before the barn had burned. Luckily, the cover had been drawn over the well, so we didn't have to shift through ash to get fresh water.

I knew I could shoot a squirrel, or a pigeon, or any number of other critters for the pot that morning. I could also go check my traps, see if there was something they'd caught. My stomach was near knotting in on itself with hunger.

But I didn't trust that look in Mama's eye. It was that crazy, long-distance stare, the one that meant she was too far gone to care about much of anything anymore. She'd be full of energy time like that, walking from one end of the woods to the other, working the still, not sleeping, barely eating. Or she might go off into town and I'd have to drag her out of jail, down from the rooftops, or once, from dancing in just her underskirt and shirtwaist on the bar in the saloon.

She told me I shouldn't mind that look too much—it was what brought me into the world.

Somehow, I didn't doubt it.

The stupid whirligig lighted next to me as I finished brewing the tea. I knew it didn't have a thought in its head. It weren't really a hound, or something intelligent. That didn't stop me from telling it, "Watch out for Mama, today." I might have hated the thing, but I still felt like I had to warn it.

No telling what Mama would do.

I'd rescued two chipped cups from the barn that morning, out back where the kitchen had been. They rinsed clean, too. I filled one with tea and brought it to Mama, making her sit down and rest for a moment.

"They got the still," she said after sipping her tea, her voice as harsh as the winter cold that would be moving in soon. "They got most of the corn meal and sugar, too. Think they dragged some of that away, before they started the fire."

That made sense. Karly and his brothers had their own still. They wouldn't need our equipment, but they would take our supplies.

"We can build a lean to, just there," Mama said, pointing away from the barn, toward one of the shorter maple trees. It was just starting to change color, from green to gold and red.

It would have been pretty if the colors hadn't made me shiver, remembering our barn, burning.

The fire hadn't been hot enough to melt metal, so we still had the heads of our tools, like axes and shovels. We'd have to shave down new handles, though, for most everything.

Mama didn't say anything else, about rebuilding the still or wondering who had done this to us. She just sat there, quiet. Before I could ask, the whirligig came flying up, brushing right past my shoulder. All the hairs on the back of my neck stood up.

Someone was coming up the trail. Damn it. My Winchester was next to the fire.

"Hey, neighbors," came a false friendly voice.

It weren't Karly and his brothers. No, it was much worse.

It was the reverend.

At Mama's behest, I made more tea and gave the reverend my cup. I wished I could have spat in it. But he had that one eye that roamed while the other looked straight ahead, and he might've seen me do it. So I didn't. His face was as pale as a frozen corpse, while his eyes was bluer than God intended the sky to be, and always looked like they was burning with rage.

The reverend sat next to Mama and talked softly to her. At least he didn't try to take her hand. I wouldn't have allowed that—might have had to accidently pour some tea down his stark black coat.

But I couldn't hear what they was saying, as Mama had sent me away, cleaning. It was a bit of a comfort that at least the whirligig stayed close to her.

Mama and the reverend had a deal about blessing the liquors we sold, and the tinctures as well. I didn't understand it, since the reverend also thought our still, and all we made, was the devil's work. Maybe he thought that praying over it would avert some of the damage we was doing, two women running a still.

The blessings might've been nice if the reverend were actually a man of the cloth. To me, though, he was just a snake, hiding in plain sight. Soon enough he'd be biting.

But he had some kind of hold over Mama. She'd listen to him when she'd never listen to anyone else. She'd even sit down to talk to him when she'd been marching here and back just moments before, walking like there were bees in her skirt.

When they'd finish their talking, she'd be blue for a day or so, not doing much of anything.

However, that was one of the reasons I tolerated the reverend. Mama would be calm for a couple weeks after their talk.

I let them have their chat, just for a bit, then I went and made up some more tea. I wouldn't have minded Mama just sitting for the rest of the day—she needed the rest. I'd had just about as much of the reverend and his dark looks as I could stand though. He always wanted me to feel guilty, just for living, and I couldn't take much of that.

And the whirligig seemed agitated as well.

I walked with the kettle back toward them, being as quiet as I could. I only heard the reverend say, "Fire ain't the only way about it, Bridget O'Malley. And the cost to your soul is so high."

That made my back bristle up. I knew the reverend thought of himself as a man of God, but he worshiped no God I recognized.

"Mama, would you like some more tea?" I asked quietly. "Or you, Reverend?"

"I was just on my way," the reverend said. Now, he did take Mama's hand. I would have smacked him if I thought I could get away with it. Even the whirligig lifted up at that, buzzing and flitting around.

Maybe it did have a thought in its mechanical head.

"Think on what I said, Bridget. God waits in judgment for all of us," he warned. "That fire was a sign, straight from Satan himself."

No, it was just business. I didn't say nothing though. Not unless I'd wanted to get myself walloped.

At least the reverend didn't try any funny stuff like kissing Mama's hand. Not even when Mama was at her lowest, sitting and not moving for days, would she have allowed that.

"It was good to see you, Reverend," I said formally, coming closer. I didn't mind if Mama called me an oaf for days, I was ready to trip and spill that hot tea all over the reverend if he didn't back up and get moving, now.

He seemed to realize there was ice under his feet. "I'll call on you ladies tomorrow," he said, letting go of Mama's hand and backing up.

The whirligig buzzed right over my shoulder. For once, that didn't make me spitting mad.

Didn't mean I still wouldn't shoot the thing first chance I got.

"We got a lot of work to do," I told the reverend. "We'll be seeing you."

The reverend fixed his one good eye on me, while the second seemed to be watching the whirligig flying behind me.

"You can be saved too," he said quietly.

I couldn't help but snort. "You sure I ain't?" I challenged him. "Now git."

I didn't have my rifle, but I was pretty sure I could take the reverend in a fair fight.

And I never fought fair.

Mama stayed blue for the rest of the day, just sitting outside the barn. I was used to that, and kept cleaning up what I could on my own. Our clothes was all burned, but I rescued more of our supplies. We'd be able to spend the night in the barn. It wouldn't be much better than sleeping out in the open, since the roof was all burned out, but I'd take what I could get.

Every once in a while I'd catch Mama looking at the barn, then out at the woods.

No matter how blue Mama was, how still she sat, I knew she was planning something.

I also knew I wasn't looking forward to finding out what.

The next morning, the gray sky looked colder than iron, rolling with clouds. I knew we'd get another downpour, maybe before lunch. We'd salvaged a few blankets—covered in pinhole burns and stinking of smoke—but at least they was warm. We sat huddled around the fire that morning, finishing the few scraps of bread that I'd scrounged.

The chicken coup had been broken into at the same time the fire had been started. I'd caught a couple that morning, but couldn't find any eggs.

However, we needed more than tea and eggs and whatever I could find for the pot. I didn't know where we was gonna get more sugar. Or the parts to build a new still. Or the coin to pay for either.

"Mama," I said quietly, not wanting to startle her. She was sitting so still that morning. "I'm gonna march over to the Holders this morning. See if I can hitch a ride into town."

I didn't mention that I'd be first gonna visit Karly.

Mama just nodded her head. "You're a good girl," she said, her jaw slack, like it got sometimes.

"I try," I told her. I may not have believed that I should live every day feeling as awful as the reverend preached that I should.

However, my gut had passed down through my boots the day before and my mood was almost as blue as Mama's.

The fire, everything, it all my fault. I shouldn't have ever gone walking through the woods with Karly. Should have kept him at a distance. Not like he'd treated me as anything other than a sister. Folks knew better than to talk, too—wouldn't want to deal with him, me, or Mama. I must have encouraged him, though, by remaining friendly.

"You remember to clean your guns," Mama instructed, like she often did. "And you keep the recipe for the best moonshine in these hills secret."

"Yes, ma'am," I told her. I didn't know why she was in such a serious mood, but at least she was talking. Sometimes when she'd get blue she'd stay silent for days.

"You know everything I could teach you," Mama said seriously. "And then some."

"Now Mama, don't be saying that," I told her sternly. I didn't need for her blue mood to go even more sour. "I could still be learning from you." I knew everything about the business, how to make the liquor and the tinctures, how to price it and bargain with the bootleggers, how to hide from the revenuers. I also knew how to shoot, better than most of the boys up here.

But I still needed to learn from her—about life, I suppose.

Not love, that weren't for either of us.

"Go on with you," Mama said. "You run into town. Go to Dickerson's Hardware and Feed. Talk with Mr. Dickerson. He's got some hardware we could use, and we could be extending him some credit."

"See Mama? That's the kind of stuff I don't know," I told her seriously. She had as many contacts in town as I did, but they was different than mine. I hadn't known we was friendly with the Dickersons. Hell, I wasn't ever sure where his store was.

Maybe Mama wasn't going to be so blue today after all. "You be sure to rest when you need to," I told her. "I don't want to come back here and find you passed out next to the fire." Mama would work her way into the grave one day, I was sure.

"Gracie O'Malley, I'm gonna take a day of rest when the good lord sees fit to come down here himself and have some tea with me," Mama said sternly.

I laughed. That was one of her usual responses.

Looked like the reverend didn't quite have his fangs in her yet.

I left the whirligig behind, telling it, "You take care of Mama. And keep an eye out. Warn her if someone's coming. You hear?"

I swear that thing bobbed up and down in the air once.

I was gonna miss it once I blasted it to pieces.

The way to Karly's homestead wasn't a well-marked path, but it was wider than a deer trail. Like us, they hid it well. Didn't want to make it too easy for the wrong types of folks to stumble over it. Even in the dim, overcast light, I could still find it—I'd walked it often enough.

Maybe a might too often.

Horsetail spikes grew up along the path, green and sharp. Wet tree leaves dripped down on my head, making me swear. I kept having to switch my rifle from one arm to the other, trying to keep it dry. Even in the thick woods, cold seeped under my sweaters, making me pull my shawl tighter across my shoulders. Damn blackberry brambles caught at my skirt. If they hadn't burned, I might have changed into pantaloons, though Mama would have thrown a fit, saying I wouldn't get any respect in them. I was too old, almost seventeen, to be wearing kids clothes.

And maybe she'd be right. Or maybe she wouldn't be. I hadn't set my mind one way or the other, yet.

After a couple miles I came to a clearing under the pines where a huge round boulder sat, like giants had been playing marbles and left one behind. I hooted twice when I saw it, as loud as I could, so the lookout would know I was coming. I was tempted to fire my rifle into the air, but that might have been announcing more of a serious visit than I wanted to pay.

Karly had enough kin to keep a guard. All Mama and I had was that damn whirligig. Which hadn't ever done us much good.

Maybe I would get us a hound, though it'd be hell to keep it out of the chickens.

I hadn't expected Karly to be the one coming around the boulder. I'd figured one of his cousins would show up first, try to scare me as usual (as if they could) then finally go off and get one of the elder boys.

Karly was about as big a man as they grew up here, at least a head taller than me, and I weren't small. He had shoulders made wide from splitting logs for the still, hands big enough to wrap around a small keg. I suppose some would have called him handsome, with big brown eyes and a ready smile. But I swear the whirligig had more thoughts running through its head than Karly did, and it showed.

"Heard about the fire," Karly said as we turned away from his family's homestead and started back up the path.

"Course you did," I told him dryly.

"Reverend came through and told us," Karly added.

"Sure," I said. "And why would he do that?" The reverend was a gossip, but he weren't trying to sweet talk any of Karly's sisters as far as I knew.

Though he was enough of a snake that maybe he was, trying to build himself a whole congregation of just women folk.

"He was trying to warn us," Karly said seriously. "Said it was a sign from God that our still was immoral."

I glanced over at Karly. He seemed sincere.

But I'd bet that even those bright, wide eyes could lie sometimes.

"Did he now," I said flatly. "Or was he just colluding with y'all? That it was just our still that was immoral? Being run by women and all." That always made me fume.

"You know I don't think that," Karly complained. "I admire you. And your mama. Running a still's hard work. And y'all have the best moonshine in these hills. Everyone knows that."

"Then why'd you burn it to the ground?" I said, stopping, finally getting to the heart of things.

Karly looked at me, startled, then he laughed and laughed, shaking his head.

I was two heartbeats away from showing him just how *dirty* I could fight, laying him out on the ground and unable to father any children.

This weren't funny.

Karly finally caught his breath. "Pa said you'd be coming. That you'd be blaming me. He ain't often right, you know, about you."

I didn't understand. Karly wasn't mad that I was accusing him, didn't seem to be taking this serious at all.

Didn't he understand that Mama would be out for more than just a pound of flesh if she found out?

"So you're telling me you and your kin didn't burn down our barn?" I asked, still not believing him.

"I swear to you, Gracie O'Malley, on my grandfather's grave, that neither I or any of my kin set fire to your barn," Karly said seriously.

Lord help me, looking into those clear, dumb eyes of his, I believed him.

"Then who did?" I asked, starting to walk again. It felt like the world was shifting under my feet, the path no longer solid. All I knew was to keep going.

"Ask the reverend," Karly said seriously. "I bet he knows."

"Why would he know?" I asked. That man was a snake, but no one would hold him close to their bosom. He was just too unsettling.

And that was saying something, considering how much I dealt with Mama.

"I know you don't care for him," Karly said. "But there's folk up here that are starting to listen to him."

I shivered. Folks up here was god fearing, but they mainly believed in a fair god. I said grace and my prayers and I worked hard. I'd been baptized and saved. I may not have been going to Heaven when I died, but that was my own doing.

I didn't need no god who told me I wasn't worth anything no matter how hard I prayed, just for being born.

Whole hills filled with folks who believed like the reverend? That weren't a pretty thought.

"Do you suppose the reverend burned our still?" I asked, trying to find my way.

"He ain't really a man of action," Karly said sincerely.

If I'd said something like that, the words would've been filled with something other than kindness.

"'Sides, I don't think he'd do anything to hurt your mama," Karly continued. "He keeps calling her the first Bride of God."

"Really?" I asked. I hadn't known that. I did know the reverend was greedy—he might've only had one good eye, but it was filled with lust when he looked at Mama.

"Says when judgment day comes, she'll be the first saved," Karly said.

"As long as she's standing beside him," I said. The reverend wasn't planning on going to Hell, that was for damn sure, though that might be the best place for him. But what did he have planned for Mama?

Karly nodded. "He ain't a bad man," he said softly. "And he'll help you, and your mama. Just like the rest of us will. We got some supplies we can spare."

"And how much is your good will gonna cost us?" I asked.

That was one thing Mama taught me early—nothing ever came for free.

"I'd just give it to you," Karly said.

"But?" I asked when he didn't go on.

"Pa wants a cut. Of your production. For the rest of the year," Karly said, his head hanging low, watching his feet, as if the path was shifting for him, too.

"Just for the rest of this year?" I asked. It was only a few months until the new year. That wouldn't be much of a run, not since we was starting from scratch.

"And a deal about the tinctures," Karly admitted. "That would be ongoing."

The herbs and medicinals was about half our business. "How big a cut?" I asked. Though I was likely to say no, it was always best to know the devil before you.

"Half," Karly said, all quiet like.

I gave one of my unladylike snorts.

"I told him that wouldn't do, that y'all would never agree," Karly said eagerly. "But he said there weren't much room left, dancing on that barrel of yours."

"Thank your pa kindly for his offer," I said, swallowing down the bitterness. We wouldn't take it—we had some leeway, like the Dickersons, that maybe he didn't know about. "But I can't decide anything on my own. I gotta go talk with Mama."

Karly sighed. "You know she's the reason why y'all got attacked, right? She's touched, Gracie. She got half the folks up here scared of what she'll do the next time she goes off."

"She's not why we was attacked," I said hotly. Mama might be difficult, but folks weren't really scared of her.

Were they?

Mama wouldn't ever hurt anyone. She'd never taken a gun when she got crazy. She knew better. And besides, I wouldn't let her. All I'd left behind at the still was the shotgun—I was carrying the rifle.

But that gave me a prickling feeling all up my spine. She'd come around from being blue pretty fast this morning.

Might mean she'd be swinging all the way around, might be at the other end by now, when the ants was crawling over her skin and she just had to move.

"I gotta go," I told Karly abruptly. "Tell your pa—tell him I believe you. That you and your family didn't set fire to our barn. But he's also gotta know what'll happen if I ever find out you're lying to me."

Karly nodded. "It'd be a blood feud, until everyone was dead."

"And beyond," I told him sincerely. "Mama's touched in more ways than one."

It weren't true, of course. Mama weren't some kind of witch, and wouldn't come after their souls. But Karly'd believe anything I told him.

"Yes, ma'am," Karly said, his big dumb eyes wide.

I knew it'd be easier if I could just go ahead and marry the stupid ox. Bring our families together.

But I'd never be settled with Karly. I'd end up going just as crazy as Mama, I just knew it.

It would be kinder to everyone if I just stayed to myself.

Still, that didn't mean my heart didn't feel a little blue as I hurried back up the path, back to that burned out wreck of a barn and whatever plans Mama had been stewing.

The sky hadn't gotten any clearer. Rain was gonna pound down, and soon. I rushed as well as I could along the path, cursing the skirt that Mama insisted I wear.

About halfway back to our homestead, I heard a buzzing like angry hornets. It was late in the season, but that didn't mean that maybe some idiot hadn't kicked over a nest. Wolf River was too far to run to if they came swarming after me. I didn't have a torch or anything to beat them off with either.

The buzzing noise got louder, then whipped around me.

Before the whirligig popped out onto the path I already had my rifle shouldered. "What the hell do you want?" I asked it.

It spun up quickly, going high, not the direction I'd been leading it.

"Damn it!" I lowered the rifle. "What do you want?" I asked again.

It buzzed down, then took off, down a deer trail to the right, toward the river.

With a sigh, I hitched up my skirt and followed it.

The path widened out after just a few feet. That didn't make no sense. Was that first narrow bit just to stop anyone from going down this way?

I pushed after the whirligig more quickly now. What had it seen? And how smart was it, really? It had always acted like just a dumb thing, following Mama everywhere, like a chick that thought she was its mama.

It weren't more than a few feet further along that I found the sugar, corn mash, yeast, and malt from our still, along with a few bags of dried herbs.

If Karly and his kin had taken our supplies, they would have brought them all the way back to their homestead. As for the reverend, well, he wouldn't have saved any of it.

And the damned whirligig only followed Mama everywhere. Not anyone else. Not ever.

Had Mama rescued some of our supplies? Before the fire? Why? What was her plan?

Or was she really as touched as everyone always said she was? Had she set the fire?

It didn't matter, not right then. The whirligig buzzed at me, and I agreed.

We needed to get back.

Whatever Mama was planning, this wasn't the half of it.

The clouds bulged full of rain and hung down low over the clearing at our homestead. I didn't see Mama near the fire, so I rushed into the barn. "Mama!" I called.

The whirligig rushed all around, searching. It's buzzing was almost a comfort, now.

Neither of us saw her, though.

Rows of neat herbs had been laid out on a table Mama had constructed out of a board and a couple logs. It looked like Mama had been getting ready to make some medicinals, maybe something for heat or the heart, I couldn't tell just from a quick glance. It would depend on the amounts, but they was all laid out in a particular order, that much I knew.

Nothing of the still remained. Even what we'd rescued was missing.

What the hell was Mama playing at? If she'd just wanted to get out of the moonshine business, all she'd have to do was tell me. I would've gladly given it up, moved onto something else.

"Hello?" came that false-friendly voice from the path.

I grabbed the rifle and marched out of the barn, aiming directly at the reverend's deceitful heart. "Give me one good reason why I don't just plug you right here, right now," I told him as I kept getting closer.

I didn't need to shorten any distance to put a hole through him. But he didn't need to know just how accurate I could be.

"Where's your mother, Grace O'Malley?" the reverend asked softly, not moving an inch.

I'll give that to the man—he weren't backing down from me.

"I was just about to ask you the same thing," I told him. "She ain't here. She's left. And I don't know where she's gone to." I didn't sound lost, or at least, that's what I told myself.

"I don't know where she is," the reverend said sincerely. Or at least as sincere as a snake can sound. "The lord moves through her sometimes, though."

I snorted. "Don't I know it." I'd been dealing with Mama and her fits all my life. I remember being barely old enough to reach her skirts and yet still having to tend to her.

But this didn't feel the same. She'd been planning something. Taking the supplies, and the still—none of that was like her.

"What kind of nonsense you been putting into her head?" I asked, not lowering my rifle at all.

"Grace O'Malley, the Word of God is not nonsense," the reverend started.

I could hear him getting wound up. "Then just tell me what you said," I told him, taking another step forward. "Tell me what you told her. Now."

"She never was baptized," the reverend said softly. "Not like you. Not like yours was proper like, but that's what she's been asking about these last few weeks. Asked me about walking into the river, having her sins washed away."

"Wolf River?" I asked.

He nodded.

"It's too swollen right now. There's been too many rains." There weren't no bridge across the river 'cause the few times someone had tried to build one, it got washed out twice a year, once in the fall and once in the spring. There was only a series of boulders, big ones, like the one marking Karly's family's territory, on either side of the most narrow bit.

I studied the reverend's face. "What ain't you telling me?" I asked. I didn't trust that smile of his, or that one wandering eye. He was a man who was born lying.

"She's been asking if the fire weren't a good baptism too," the reverend admitted. "Wanted to know if it was a good first step, going through the fire, then the water, to really wash all her sins away."

Shit. Mama really had lost it, hadn't she?

"So she's been asking you about fire for some time now?" I said, taking one more step closer, the muzzle of the barrel brushing against his raven black coat.

That meant she must have been the one to start the fire.

The reverend's good eye wouldn't meet mine. He just nodded his head. "Aye."

"Then we better get us to the river," I said. "See if we can't save her from herself."

"I didn't encourage her," the reverend assured me. "Not like that."

I knew he was lying. He was probably the one to put the idea of fire into her head in the first place. Burn down our still, save us from ourselves. Separate us from our livelihood, make us dependent on him.

But I couldn't take care of the reverend. Not yet. Not until after we went and rescued Mama from herself.

"Let's go," I said, shouldering my rifle. "Come on!" I called to the whirligig.

The herbs Mama had put out made sense now. They was for fighting off the cold, clearing the lungs.

And we was all gonna need it, because just then the clouds opened and rain started pouring down.

I couldn't see more than a few feet in front of my face—everything beyond that was just a sheet of water, messy and hidden. Couldn't hear the whirligig either, though I knew it was up ahead. For once, I understood what the reverend meant by having to bow my head before God and the power of nature. The wind was fierce and the rain pounding down.

But I wasn't about to stop. We slogged our way along the path, slipping in the mud more than once. I knew I was a sight, hair bedraggled, covered in filth, shaking with cold.

Mama was up ahead, however.

We came out of the woods near the crossing, where the large rocks marked the edges.

However, I could barely see the boulders. Roaring water came nearly to the top of the far ones, and at least halfway up the ones closest to us.

I'd never seen Wolf River so wild and irate. It sounded like one of those trains full of coal from the mountains, rushing so fast nothing was stopping it.

"Mama!" I called. I knew it was useless—nobody could hear nothing in that storm.

The whirligig came buzzing right up to me. I only heard it because it was barely an inch from my face. Then it flew off, over the river.

I followed it to the best of my abilities. Then I saw it. In the middle of the river there was a dark spot.

A head of hair as black as mine.

Mama.

The whirligig danced above the spot for a few moments, then bounced along, like it was skipping over the wild water, up to the closest boulder, circling it.

Right at the top, when the river took a breath, I saw a rope tied around the top of the rock.

Seemed Mama weren't completely crazy. She'd done tied herself to the boulder before going into the water.

But the water had ahold of her now, and she couldn't make her way back. If she was even alive and hadn't frozen herself to death. I'd only been in the rain and I was already shivering so hard I couldn't make myself stand still.

I marched over to the reverend, getting close to him. Even with the rain washing him clean I could still smell the sourness on him, his teeth rotting, his gut spoiled. "Mama's out there!" I shouted. "Follow the whirligig!"

The reverend looked out over the water, his good eye catching hold of the brass critter.

At least he was smart enough to see Mama's predicament.

"I'll fetch her," the reverend told me. "You go get help!"

"From where?" I asked him. We was miles away from the nearest farmstead. Besides that, no one would come.

"Have faith," the reverend said. "Mine will carry me through."

He marched past me, heading straight for the water.

Damn fool was gonna get himself killed as well.

"Don't!" I shouted, pulling him back by his shoulder. "The water will wash you away before you get to her," I pointed out.

"Have faith," he repeated. Even though he was shouting, the words still came out gentle like.

The reverend took off, as if those devils he was always chasing were finally chasing him. With a mighty leap, the reverend jumped up, landing on top of the first boulder marking the edge of the river. He tilted for a moment, but he kept to his feet.

I knew the pattern of the boulders, how they marched out into the river. Seemed the reverend did too. It only took him three more jumps to get to the one tied to Mama.

Well, if he could do that, then so could I. I gathered my skirts together, about to race up like the reverend had.

Before I could take a single step, though, the damn whirligig appeared right in front of my face, making me startle like a spring hare.

"Damn it! I need to go help!" I yelled at the thing.

It just buzzed at me, not letting me go.

I looked out at the reverend. He'd laid down on the boulder that Mama was tied to, and was tugging on the rope. The water surged over his legs and back, but he held on, not letting it take him.

Mama's bobbing head started moving away from the center of the river and toward the safety of the rocks.

Maybe the reverend didn't need help, from me or any distant neighbor. Maybe he could rescue Mama. I sure didn't want to be beholden to him, but if he saved her, I'd swallow my pride and think more kindly of him.

Mama came closer and closer. I saw her stick a hand up out of the water, reaching for the reverend. Their fingers touched.

Then the reverend was in the water.

Mama's dark head bobbed beside his as they tumbled down the stream. Seemed the rope had come undone.

The whirligig bobbed above their heads as they were swept away by the river.

"No!" I screamed. I ran as fast as I could down the side of the river, trying to keep up.

But the water was too wild, eating up too much of the bank. I couldn't keep up, not on dry land. And if I stepped into the river, I'd be swept away too.

Mama and the reverend quickly passed out of view.

The bodies of both the reverend and Mama washed up a few miles downstream, tangled together in the rope that had been holding Mama to the boulder.

Made me wonder all over again what Mama had been planning.

Had she set the fire? Had she meant to take the reverend with her in the water? I remembered her talk that last day. Was she really just touched? I'd like to believe that maybe she was trying to save us all, but Mama wasn't kind that way.

Damned whirligig never returned either. Don't know if it got caught in the storm as well, or if it just run off.

I buried Mama opposite the remains of the barn at the farmstead, away from the well. Karly and two of his brothers came by and helped me dig the hole. It was dirty, smelly work, particularly with the ground so wet. We all looked like spooks by the time we was finished, heads and hands and arms and legs all covered in mud.

Mama's face held a frozen, wild look, even with the river bloat. I kept a cloth over it, not wanting folks to say anything during the funeral. Not that many came. I didn't expect much of anyone besides Karly and his brothers.

One of the bootleggers showed up, though, supposedly to pay respects. He was a tall man, with a big barrel chest and white hair. Seemed a bit old for a bootlegger, but maybe he was the boss or something. He introduced himself as Old Henry. Karly just nodded at him, seeming to recognize him, and that was good enough for me.

I didn't trust Old Henry's shifty eyes, though. He was just sniffing around to see about production, I suspected.

There weren't much to say as I put Mama in the ground. "She tried her best," I told the five bowed heads. "And now God's granting her a grace that she's always been missing."

"Amen," they intoned.

Didn't take near as long to bury her. Then Karly, his three brothers, and the bootlegger all left, and I was by myself on the farmstead.

I dug up a couple of jugs that Mama had put away, special. The clouds had finally passed and the full moon came up cold and harsh. Winter was on its way.

I sat down next to the grave, leaning my back against a tree with my rifle at hand, as I took my first drink. Then I poured one over the grave, sharing with Mama as we always had. I wasn't sure what I was doing next, except taking another drink.

Did I want to stay in the hills? Hire me some help and get the still going again? It was a thought. But without Mama, the idea of running the still on my own just didn't appeal.

Was there something I could do in town? Some kind of work that a single, unmarried woman could do that wouldn't leave too bad a taste in my mouth? I wouldn't be no good as a nanny or a cook, that was for damned sure. And I didn't want to whore myself out at the saloon.

I sure as hell wasn't about to marry Karly, though that seemed to be the path he and his family thought I should take.

Instead, I took another drink. Then I slowly put it down and put my hand on my rifle.

Something had just set all the hairs up along the back of my neck. A sound that didn't belong to the night wind and the trees with their few leaves.

That damned bootlegger, Old Henry, came creeping back up along the trail. Luckily, since most of the trees was bare, the clearing on our homestead was open, and the moon was shining down nicely.

I stayed where I was, playing possum. Gave out a quiet snore. Let him think I'd drank myself foolish.

I wasn't sure what Old Henry was looking for. All the account books had burned—not that it mattered, because I kept all the numbers in my head. We didn't ever have much on hand.

Bootlegger barely glanced in my direction before heading off to the barn. He had a revolver in his hand, at the ready.

What the hell was going on?

Didn't take Old Henry long. Saw him coming back out with a bag. Must have been buried, as he was brushing dirt from the side of it.

What had Mama been doing with this bootlegger? Had she buried something for him? Or told him about something when she'd been feeling wild?

Then I heard a click and whirl, followed by a quiet buzzing.

Had the damned whirligig come back?

But it weren't ours, no. It was shorter and round. It was Old Henry's own whirligig.

Maybe this Old Henry had been the one Mama had stolen ours from.

I rolled to my side, sliding off the tree I'd been leaning against, as if I was asleep. The bootlegger bought the act.

He couldn't see me too well laying on the ground, all in shadows, couldn't see me get up on my elbows, rifle in hand.

Couldn't see me take aim and shoot. I followed the sound of his whirligig, not relying on my eyes.

Got the stupid thing in one. Parts spewed all over the place. It was damned satisfying.

"Don't shoot!" Old Henry cried out. He held both his gun and his stolen bag over his head.

I rolled out of the shadows and stood up in the light, holding my rifle steady. I didn't have to come no closer to kill him right quick, and he knew it.

"Whatcha got there?" I asked him.

"My own property," Old Henry said stubbornly. "Your Mama was just holding it for me."

"So why'd you come back like a thief? Why not just ask me for it?" I pointed out reasonably.

"Miss O'Malley, would you have believed me?" he asked.

He had a point.

"I believe we've gotten off on the wrong foot," Old Henry said. He stood up straighter and his accent cleared up. He sounded more like the town folk all of a sudden. "I am Henry Dickerson, at your service."

Mama had told me to go into town and seek out this Mr. Dickerson.

"So why don't you show me what you got there?" I said, drawing closer.

"I'll toss the bag to you. Ready?" he asked, his voice soft and easy.

I knew it could be a trick. He could throw that bag right in my face. I still let him toss it to me, keeping my eyes, and my gun, on him the whole time.

The bag held a couple of pincers that would have fit our departed whirligig, as well as some other spare parts that I assumed were for it. There were only a couple of coins in the bottom of the bag that I slid into my shirt. Better for me to have them than him.

"So what were you and Mama up to?" I asked, tossing the bag back to him.

"Your mama was smarter than she let on," Mr. Dickerson said. "She had an affinity for automatons."

"For what?"

"Machines. Like the one that you had. That the parts in this bag were for," he said.

"The whirligig," I told him. Maybe that was why Mama wanted me to shoot the thing. So she could get some practice replacing the parts on it.

"Yes. The whirligig. Your mama was wanting to get out of the moonshine business. Feared that it wasn't going to be safe for too long. So I was teaching her automatronics, how to make and fix machines," Mr. Dickerson explained.

That may have been what Mama was planning—to get us both out of the hills. Or maybe not. Maybe she'd just been crazy.

But whatever she'd been planning didn't matter anymore.

I had to make my own plans.

"You know I'm smarter than I let on as well," I told Mr. Dickerson.

"So I've heard, Miss O'Malley," Mr. Dickerson said gravely. "Your mama was always bragging on you, and how you could add any numbers together in your head, even ones she'd never heard of. You also kept all the accounts straight, never having to write anything down."

"Reckon that's all true," I told him. I'd never learned to read—I'd always had to keep everything in my head. "I figure I could learn that automatronics as well," I added boldly. I'd always hated that whirligig, but maybe it could help me finally. "Could learn to make and fix machines. Like Mama was."

Mr. Dickerson broke into a huge smile, his teeth flashing white in the moonlight. "Why Miss. O'Malley, I thought you'd never ask. I'd be happy to take you on as an apprentice at my shop."

Apprentice? That might mean moving into town, and out of the hills.

That sounded like a better plan than any of the other choices I'd been facing.

"Deal," I said, lowering my rifle.

"Your first task will be rebuilding my own—what did you call it? Whirligig."

That sounded fair to me.

Then I could build one of my own.

And shoot it.

I started this story three times. Each time, I got several thousand words in, then had to throw out everything I'd done and start again. I'd written two other Gracie stories, and I just couldn't find the start of this one. I had Gracie in town, first, then on the railroad (where she meets the professor) then at a mine— none of them worked.

I finally got Gracie into Mr. Dickerson's shop. But this story went in fits and starts. I finished it over the course of a weekend. I wouldn't say I struggled with it, but I think I probably wrote an extra 5000 words that I ended up not using by the time I was done, scenes that I cut or that just wouldn't work.

I still like where this story ended up. And I have a very good idea about the next Gracie story, chronologically speaking.

GRACIE BREAKS OUT

Whirl-clank. Whirl-clank.

I couldn't for the life of me figure out what kind of contraption was making such a racket out in the front of Mr. Dickerson's Hardware and Feed store. I put the toy mouse I was fixing down on the wooden workbench, next to the fine-edged tweezers I was using to set the spring right, then leaned back on my hard stool, listening in the still summer afternoon, surrounded by all the machines and parts, the repair room smelling like oil and metal shavings.

Whirl-clank. Whirl-clank.

Now, Mr. Dickerson had told me more than once that my place was in the back of the store, hidden away in the repair room. He'd have me coming in after closing if he could—he never wanted no customers seeing me.

Didn't want no one to have any idea that a woman were fixing their automatons.

However, Mrs. Bailey had strict rules about the hours good girls kept and when I could be coming and going from her Boarding House for Proper Ladies. So I worked regular like, when the store was open.

I'd run into this some when I'd been living in the hills with Mama, before I'd come down into Hortonsville. Horrible worse it was here. Made me just want to spit some days instead of smiling and playing like a nice girl.

Made me wonder if this was how Mama went crazy. Why she ended up in the hills.

But no matter how often Mr. Dickerson told me to stay in the back, I was always finding some excuse to go up front.

Bastard knew better than to crop my wages. Most everything'd stopped working 'round here the one time he'd tried it.

Whirl-clank-clank.

It had to be some kind of special machine. I bet it was some new inventor, too.

I just had to see.

I didn't flaunt myself, though. I checked the doorway first, making sure no one'd be tracking which direction I'd be coming from.

Not a soul in sight.

I slipped up the first aisle, mainly filled with replacement parts for steam-powered farm machinery, like shakers and fanners for the thrashers, new blades for the reapers, as well as old-fashioned rakes and hoes. Then I made a beeline for the millet and corn—easy enough to explain I'd been sent there to fetch something for my non-existent husband if someone asked.

Finally, I wound my way around to the front, where the automaton parts was kept: shelves of brass gears and iron plates, gold filaments and wire, lenses and sturdy leathers.

Close to the front of the shop, the aisles opened up. In front of the wooden counter a wide space had been cleared for customers to bring their gizmos and whirligigs and whatever other machines they had that needed fixing.

Three men stood around an odd, four-legged critter. Mr. Dickerson still stood behind the counter, stroking his white moustache with one hand while keeping the other wrapped around his barrel chest. He wore his usual red wool vest, black pants, and white shirt. He looked like the grand gentleman, about to pass wise judgment.

Oh, he knew his automatons and whirligigs, but he were merely a tinker, like myself. Neither of us were really the inventing sort.

We'd both been trying. Give me a set of schematics and I could build any machine laid out.

I'd never been able to create something outta nothing, though.

Two of the three other men wore dark brown coats and vests, with lighter brown pants—typical for the men of Hortonsville—though I'd only seen one of them before. He owned one of the local mercantile stores, not the good one on Main Street, but the one across the river that would sell a brush made of cheap horse hair claiming it had good boar's bristles. A stuffy mustache covered the bottom half of his face, probably trying to make up for his pear-shaped gut. The other looked almost like his brother, except his eyes was even more weasely and he were clean-shaven.

The third man wore a long tan coat that had tails, with a gray vest and matching pants. A white silk scarf hung long around his neck, and he wore a black top hat. Even from where I was standing, I could see his clear, piercing blue eyes following the mechanical critter and its halting step.

It was the size of the card tables they had down at Anderson's Pleasure Hall. A black iron see-saw—looking like it was made for kids—stuck out of the top of it, probably a mechanical power source. It was mostly wood above. Below, it had four legs made from differing lengths of iron pipe and ending with wheels.

They was what was making that great clanking sound, when they touched the wooden floor.

The front two glided along just fine, but the back two were built like the hind legs of a horse. One was bending backwards, then stepping down. The table top lurched as it found its new balance.

"It's just so—inelegant," the well-dressed man complained. "The legs are efficient, and will move the mechanism out of harm's way. But I think I must add a gyroscope or something to make the movement more smooth."

Mr. Dickerson grunted wisely.

He didn't have a clue what the gentleman was talking about.

I rolled my eyes. "Y'all could just change the gear ratio," I said, stepping forward.

I knew it weren't my place to say nothing. Gyroscopes was damned expensive. Even if the fancy gentleman did look as though he could afford it.

Not that I was trying to take business away from Mr. Dickerson. He'd been good to me. Mostly. And when other people wasn't around, he treated me all right.

Maybe I was showing off, just a bit.

"How so?" the young man asked, looking directly at me.

The two locals gave me a kind smile—the sort they'd give to a child. They obviously didn't expect me to say anything intelligent.

"Change the twenty-tooth sprocket to an eighteen," I suggested. "Then adjust the belt mechanism, here, and here," I showed him on the nearby leg.

"It'll make the automaton slower," the gentleman said, considering.

"Of course it would," Mr. Dickerson said, as if he had any idea of what the gentleman meant.

The local store owner said, "Maybe if you increased the sprocket size…"

I coulda told the store owner that he was being stupid. If anything, I would have dropped the sizes right down and added another gear instead.

I didn't say nothing though. I'd had my say.

Mr. Dickerson might be mad I'd showed up, but he might not be, if he got to haggling ratios with these three for a while.

I turned to go, but before I could escape back into the repair room, the young gentleman said, "Excuse me, miss."

I stopped. Damn it. Mr. Dickerson was going to be right furious if a customer took offense at a woman offering advice.

"Yes?" I asked, just turning my head.

"I know I'm being awfully forward," the gentleman said, "But could you do me the honor of sharing your name?"

Mr. Dickerson huffed behind the counter. "This here's Miss O'Malley."

The gentleman stepped closer, holding out his hand.

He didn't expect me to curtsey, did he? That weren't something I'd ever mastered, no matter how many time Mrs. Bailey had been trying to teach me.

I turned, though, and held out my hand as well.

"Professor Sigler, and my magnificent automatons, at your service," he said as he took my hand in his and bowed his head over it. His hand felt soft against my rough palm, and warmer than any fire.

The professor held my hand a moment longer than was proper, his clear eyes sparkling down at me. And I weren't no small and delicate lady.

"Professor," I said, drawing my hand back, feeling my heart pounding like one of those foolish school girls at the boarding house who'd just left home for the first time.

"Miss O'Malley, might I have the honor of calling on you for lunch sometime?" the professor asked

I looked over at Mr. Dickerson. I never took no lunch. I just worked through the day. Might eat something over the workbench, if I'd brought it.

However, Mr. Dickerson was smiling like a proud papa. "I think that'd do nicely," he said. "You can come calling here tomorrow, take her someplace nice."

"Noon, tomorrow, then," Professor Sigler said, tipping his hat to me.

"All right," I said. "Goodbye."

"Goodbye, Miss O'Malley," the professor said in a voice that promised…something.

I turned and hurried back to the rear of the shop. I sure weren't blushing—I weren't the blushing type.

But my insides were churning up like I'd taken a gulp of Mama's purest moonshine.

I told myself not to pay no attention. I'd been living with silly girls for more'an three years now, girls who couldn't shoot and wouldn't be able to tell good moonshine from piss water.

Sure, I remembered what it was like to first move into town, how I'd gaped like the hillbilly I'd been the first time I'd seen the electric street lights. Hell, Mrs. Bailey'd had to teach all of us how to use that new-fangled indoor plumbing she'd just installed.

I weren't like them, though. I'd been on my own for a long while, taking care of Mama when she weren't able to take care of herself, running the still up in the hills until she'd died, then coming down here into town and learning automatons and gizmos and gears and such. I had a career, as such, as much as a woman could, hiding behind Mr. Dickerson, the owner of the store.

It was better than when I'd been in the hills.

But I still yearned for something different.

Not like those stupid settlers who thought the far side of the country were gonna be the Promised Land. People was people, and there'd still be folks and towns and everything else on the other side of those long rails stretching from New York City to California.

Didn't mean I weren't hankering to go join them sometimes.

Westward, always westward—had heard that often enough. Felt like the train whistles sang those words at night, carrying them far on the winds.

And maybe, just maybe, this gentleman felt the same way. Could be he could see a woman and know she had some worth. Maybe he were different than the folks here.

Different enough to shake me loose.

Lights out at the boarding house was supposed to be around seven o'clock at night during the cold of winter—I figure it was to save Mrs. Bailey on the expense of wood and oil. During the summer, the rules was relaxed, mainly 'cause the sun gave us all the light we needed, up 'til ten o'clock through July and August. Mrs. Bailey still might fuss a bit, but as long as I was up at sunrise and ready to help with the cooking for the other boarders and doing my chores, she let me be.

I'd already changed outta my day dress—and that damned corset—and into the only decent nightgown I had, made from white cotton, soft and loose. It were the most comfortable thing I owned. I had more outfits in my dresser than I think all the folks up the hills had in their possession, combined—hell, I even had two fancy dresses for church, and another one, just for holidays!

Fortunately, Mr. Dickerson understood that I needed to move my arms, so he didn't care if I weren't the most fashionably dressed, or if my corset weren't cinched as tightly as it could be.

Still hated the damned thing, and would have burned it if I could.

I sat up in my bed in my corner room, looking at a set of schematics that Mr. Dickerson had "loaned" me, though he didn't know he had. They was for a different type of whirligig—a fancy *ornithopter*, from France, or so Mr. Dickerson had told me.

I couldn't read the directions none—Mama had never taught me my letters—so I had a lot of conjecture about the types of materials they was using. Still, I reckoned it wouldn't be too hard build a model. I had some scraps saved away, left over gears and wire, and I could always barter away some time with Mr. Dickerson for the rest of what I needed.

It weren't original work, but it might be close enough that Mr. Dickerson could sell some of 'em under his own name.

As I expected, a timid knock sounded on my door just before the night bells sounded.

"Come on in," I called out, folding up the papers and setting them aside.

Mildred poked her head in. "Are you—Oh!" she exclaimed when she saw what I was wearing.

"Just get in here," I told her, patting the bed.

"But you're undressed!" she complained. She still came in and shut the door behind her.

"It ain't nothing you ain't seen before," I pointed out. "Hell, you even own a pair yourself."

"Grace O'Malley," Mildred said sternly as she walked across the room, keeping her eyes on the floor. "It still isn't proper."

I shrugged, though I knew she couldn't see me. "Don't care." And I really didn't. I didn't see why I couldn't dress like how I liked in my own room.

Didn't think God cared, either, as long as I said my prayers, went to church on Sundays, and generally tried, well, not to be good, but not to be too bad, either.

Mildred sat down on the bed, not looking at me, still in her prim black dress. She were a mousy thing, with mousy brown hair all pulled back and washed-out brown eyes, the color of an old mud stain on pale sheets.

"So how was your day?" I finally asked when all Mildred did was sit there and wring her hands.

"I don't know, Grace," she said with a sigh. "I'm just not getting the hang of it."

Mildred worked as a clerk at an office, where they was trying to teach her how to use one of those new typing machines. She knew her letters and she loved to read— sometimes on a Sunday afternoon, after church, we'd sit in the garden out back of the boarding house and she'd read out loud to the rest of us, poems and stories and the bible, of course.

Typing was hard work, though. The operator of the machine couldn't see what words they was coming up with, not until they'd finished a full line.

I'd tried to help, but Mildred didn't have clever fingers. We'd joked that if we could take her reading and my hands we'd make a complete office clerk.

"I'm sure you'll get it," I told her, though I weren't sure at all. Mildred had a name that didn't fit her. I'd tried calling her Millie, but just once. We were alike, that way—I sure weren't full of God's light, any more than she had strength and fortitude of will, gentle or no.

"I have some news," I told her. I didn't know if it'd cheer her up or not. "There was a young inventor in the store today."

"Really?" Mildred looked up at that. "Was he handsome?"

I snorted. "I suppose. In a fancy, dressed up way."

I remembered how soft his hand had felt in mine and got that funny feeling in my stomach again.

"He were having no luck with this machine of his. So I showed him how to change the gear ratio." I was still pleased with that.

"You didn't!" Mildred said, shocked. "I don't know how you find the nerve to stand up to men—and complete strangers even—like that." She folded her arms over her stomach suddenly, as if she were protecting herself.

"It weren't much," I told her. "But he seemed impressed. Asked me my name."

Damn it, why the hell did I remember every word he'd said, and how he'd be honored?

"Wants to come calling, take me to lunch," I said in a rush.

I don't know why Mildred suddenly looked so pale. Were she coming down with something?

"Oh!" Mildred exclaimed. "That's wonderful news! You have a gentleman courter!" She straightened up suddenly, and gave me a smile that weren't real.

"I don't think he's to the courting stage, yet," I told her, maybe a bit harshly.

Maybe telling myself that as well.

"But he's taking you to lunch? Where? What are you going to wear?" Mildred asked.

"Mr. Dickerson instructed him to take me somewheres nice," I told her. "I ain't thought about my dress." I didn't know I should have.

"I know which one," Mildred said, jumping up off the bed and going over to my dresser. She threw open the door and picked out my good Friday dress, the one I only wore when I was mainly in the shop and not in the back. "This one," she announced firmly.

It were made from patterned cotton—pale green with white stripes—and a white linen collar and cuffs. The sleeves was too puffy at the top, too tight at the bottom, for me to move comfortable in.

But it cut in on the sides, showing off my waist, then out, over my hips, and it were a bit low in the front too, not going all the way up my neck like most of my new dresses.

"All right," I said, watching her hang it up on the door of the wardrobe. "I'll wear that one."

"Good," Mildred said, turning back to me. She smiled, then realized that she were looking me in the eye and looked down at the floor again.

"Wanna see what I was studying?" I asked, bringing back out the schematics.

"Now Grace, you know I can't make heads or tails of such things," Mildred complained, but she came back over and perched on the side of my bed anyway.

"It's an *ornithopter*," I told her, proud of the new word I'd learned.

"My goodness!" Mildred said, tracing her finger over the drawings.

"It's just a different type of whirligig," I told her. "But instead of four or six wings, they'se trying to make do with just two."

"Do you really think you could build such a thing?" Mildred asked.

"Of course," I bragged. And maybe I could, and maybe I couldn't. It would depend on how far from the original drawings I'd have to go.

"I just don't see how you'd do it," Mildred said, looking at the view that had all the pieces separated out. "I don't see how you'd put them together."

"I ain't hard," I assured her. "It's just a knack, of seeing the parts and then seeing them whole." I'd learned early that all the inventors who came to the store could not only do this, but a lot more, changing a gear in their heads to change the whole gizmo. I could do some of that, but not like the really good professors.

However, that gave me an idea. I scrambled out of bed and to my desk, pulling out one of my many failed drawings and a pencil. The back of the paper was at least clean.

I sat back down on the bed and made a line of circles across the paper, spacing them out evenly, stopping after ten. Then I handed the pencil to Mildred.

"What are the letters of the typing machine? The first line?" I asked. "Do you know them?"

She nodded slowly.

"Write 'em down. One in each circle," I instructed.

Mildred filled each circle.

"Now do the next line," I told her.

She filled out three lines of letters, plus some other characters I didn't know.

"You said you can't figure out where to put your hands, can't see the letters," I told her. "So how about using this for practice?" Maybe the spacing was wrong, but at least it was a start. It would let her see how to type.

Mildred put the paper down on the bed, flexed her hands, then started pressing her fingers against the different letters.

"I don't know if I'm doing it right," she complained. "There's no line at the end."

I shrugged. "But at least it's a way to practice," I pointed out. "Might help you get better." I didn't know how else she was gonna learn, if she couldn't see the letters or the machine in her head, and couldn't get her fingers to move the right way.

"Thank you," Mildred said after practicing moving her fingers for another few moments. "I think—I think this may work."

"You're welcome," I told her.

The night vesper bells rang from St. Luke's down the street. Mildred stood up immediately.

"Take that with you," I told her. "You keep practicing. You can do this."

Mildred looked up at me again. "Thank you. I don't know what I'd do without you here."

I didn't know either. "You'll find your strength," I assured her. That were the sort of things friends was supposed to say to each other, right?

"And you'll find the light of god," Mildred replied, as always. She paused, then pointed to the schematics I'd pushed to the side, "If you want, I'll read the notes to you sometime."

"That'd be right fine," I told her. It weren't that I was ashamed of not being able to read, but I still didn't ever bring it up none.

Besides, I could still add together more numbers and fix more things than any of the fancy bankers and clerks in town.

"Good night, Grace," Mildred said at the door.

"Sweet dreams, Mildred," I told her. After she'd gone, I lay down on my bed and looked over at the dress hanging on the wardrobe door.

It weren't right, me being so excited to go out to lunch with this professor. Then again, there were folks in town who'd say it weren't right for me to be fixing their gizmos and automatons, that all a girl was good for was making babies and taking care of the home.

I knew that this professor didn't believe that. He believed a woman could do more.

And maybe that's what excited me most of all.

I weren't about to pay any attention to the time the next morning after I got to Mr. Dickerson's Feed and Hardware store, or at least that's what I told myself.

No watching the clock and sighing like those foolish schoolgirls who'd been at the boarding house last summer.

The day were gonna be a day like every other that summer, sunny that morning with a good wind coming down off the hills and stirring up all the dust in the street, with hopefully a shower that afternoon to settle everything down.

Two new machines was waiting for me on the bench that morning: A wood-and-brass clockwork horse that had been wound too tight, along with a fancy-painted, gold-and-white ball. I put that to the side, figuring Mr. Dickerson would like to try his hand first. I also slipped the plans away, on the side, so he'd never know I'd had 'em.

The horse was simple enough to take apart. I was cleaning and polishing every gear when Mr. Dickerson finally showed up.

"Morning Gracie," he said as he came in the back, hanging up his jacket and hat, wearing his usual red vest and black trousers. His white hair lay plastered across his skull, but it was starting to curl up at the tops of his ears—he'd have to get it cut again soon. "Are you all ready for your luncheon date?"

"I suppose," I told him. I didn't want to sound too eager. It was gonna be too easy to get a heaping lot full of disappointment if I weren't careful.

I'd tied my leather work apron higher that morning so I'd cover more of my dress. I didn't want to get oil or nothing on it. I was moving more slow, too—but that at least was in part because the damned sleeves limited my reach.

Mr. Dickerson knew better, though. "Would you like to know more about the professor?" he asked, his gray eyes twinkling over his big white mustache.

"All right," I said, putting down the machinery I'd been working on with a bit too much force, making a loud clank in the quiet morning. "Tell me about him." I wanted to learn everything I could about the professor, but it weren't my place to ask, or so I'd been told by Mildred that morning.

"I wouldn't have suggested he take you to lunch without knowing his character," Mr. Dickerson told me earnestly. "Professor Sigler is a fine inventor. He's here on business, staying at the Fremont hotel. He checked in a week ago, and is paid up in advance for a few more weeks."

That was interesting to me. "Where's he from?" I asked. He didn't have a local accent, but it didn't sound like he was from New York City either.

"Went to school in Indiana," Mr. Dickerson said, warming to the subject. "That fancy engineering college out there."

"Really?" I asked. Why the hell did that make my breath catch? Just because he was good looking and smart didn't mean nothing. "Did he teach out there too?"

"Not sure where he's been teaching," Mr. Dickerson said, looking thoughtful. "That's something you can ask him at your lunch."

I couldn't stop myself from looking up at the grandfather clock sitting and ticking quietly in the corner. It was only a little after eight.

I was never gonna make it 'til noon.

"His parents still have property, down the coast some, in Virginia," Mr. Dickerson. "His older brothers took over the farm, but the professor, he wanted to go see the bright lights."

I couldn't help but sigh. I knew all about wanting to see those lights. The ones here in Hortonsville wouldn't compare to those in New York City.

I wanted to see those lights too.

"He's always been inventing, tinkering. He really liked your suggestion of the differing gears. Of course, he made some more adjustments, but he thinks the new version is going to be just what he needs."

"Of course," I said dryly. Even if the professor had taken everything I said to heart, Mr. Dickerson wouldn't ever have given me credit. "What's it for, anyway?"

"It's some kind of traveling machine," Mr. Dickerson said, waving his hand.

That made me raise an eyebrow. Either Mr. Dickerson really didn't know, or the professor had told him and he hadn't understood it.

Interesting.

"Did you take a look at the boulette?" Mr. Dickerson asked, walking over to the bench and picking up the fancy ball.

"Left that for you," I told him honestly.

"Let me show you how it comes apart," he said, drawing up his own stool.

Though I mighta been able to figure it out on my own, I was grateful for Mr. Dickerson to be showing me, to give me a distraction, something to think about other than how slow the clock was moving, how many hours and minutes it'd be until noon.

Around eleven thirty, Mr. Dickerson had me stop and go wash up behind the store. He even let me use the buttermilk soap after brushing under my nails with the tar-based bar, so my hands smelled clean and not like machine oil.

Though somehow, I doubted the professor would have minded me smelling like well-oiled machinery.

Then I went and waited behind the counter, without my worker apron, like I was a good shop girl or clerk. Mr. Dickerson didn't generally put me out there. I could add up a man's bill fast enough, but I'd struggle writing him out a receipt.

The professor came in the door right as the Eastern Pennsylvania Railroad blew its noon whistle. He wore a gray long coat with matching gray trousers and a black-and-gray-striped vest.

I hoped my own plain dress didn't give him no shame.

"Miss O'Malley," he said as he came up to the counter, holding out his hand again.

I gave him mine, not letting my fingers shake none. He didn't kiss the back of my hand, though he was thinking about it, I could tell. Just squeezed my fingers against his soft skin, then let go.

Not sure how I would have reacted if he'd tried, though. Mama would have walloped him but good for being so forward.

I came around the counter to stand next to him. It was just so odd to be looking up at a man—mostly I either looked 'em eye-to-eye, or even down at them.

It took me a moment to realize that he'd crooked his elbow out and expected me to tuck my hand there.

Made my stomach do all that flipping nonsense again.

I shook myself, took his elbow, and let him lead me out of the shop. "How's your morning been?" I asked as he opened the door for me and we stepped into the bright sunlight.

"Fair to middling," he said as he offered his arm again.

At least this time I seen it. I took it gratefully, though I knew that would be setting all the tongues in the town wagging after me.

The professor told me about a new machine he was inventing, some kind of flying machine that had a light on it.

"An ornithopter?" I asked, pleased that I could maybe use some of his language, and not just the words I knew from the hills.

The professor stopped dead in the middle of the broad walk. "Miss O'Malley, you are truly a treasure," he said. He lifted his hat to me, then started us walking again. "I'd been pondering the wing ratios, and how to fit four tiny wings onto the back of the luminescent element I'd had in mind. An ornithopter, with its simple two wings, is exactly the answer I was seeking! Thank you, my dear."

"You're welcome," I said. Mama may not have taught me much manners, but I at least knew that.

He kept talking about his machine and I tried to follow along. The problem was I had to see it—down on paper— before I could really have a good idea. I just always had troubles picturing everything in my head like a proper inventor.

We stroll down to the Smithton Inn. I'd never been there before, but I'd seen it. I'd walked by it one night, last Christmas, looking in the windows at all the starched, white-linen tablecloths and glass chandeliers, the ladies in their fancy colored silks with bare shoulders, and the gentlemen in their tails and striped shirts.

I mighta trembled, just a bit, as we waited on the threshold for a waiter to come and take us to our table. It was a big room, with white tablecloths and heavy, green-velvet chairs. Fine folks sat and drank from crystal glasses and had tinkling laughs.

This was far fancier than any place I'd ever been.

"You'll do fine," the professor whispered, patting my hand just before the waiter came back.

How much did he know about me? Wouldn'ta been hard to learn, I suppose, that I'd come down outta the hills. I'd done well for myself, though, better than most folks.

But I still had the hills in my heart.

Luckily, I didn't trip or nothing as we walked across that open space. The waiter was in a black vest and tie, with a white shirt and apron. He plucked up a card off the table before pulling out the chair for me.

I sat, trying for dainty but I suspect missing by a mile.

After the professor sat down across the table from me, he told me, "I had them reserve this table, just for us."

"Thank you," I told him. It was a nice table, right at the window. We was up above the street and had a good view of the folks walking by. Every type of person seemed to be on the broadwalk that afternoon: Fine ladies in silks and gloves with their matching gentlemen; a gang of street children with their dirty hands and faces, racing after an unknown prize; mid-level clerks and secretaries, hurrying to their dinner; even a fancy inventor, wearing goggles and a leather work apron, cradling a still steaming gizmo that had melted in on itself.

We could also see the street and the fancy open carriages just for town trips with the horses kicking up dust. At least two steam-powered machines drove by, huffing and puffing as they rolled along.

The waiter poured us water in fresh glasses, sparkling like everything else in the room, then handed us each a stiff board with lots of writing on it. It also had numbers—prices, I guessed. I could make out some of those, adding them up in my head.

This meal was gonna cost more than I made in a month.

The professor looked carefully at the board in his hand. I pretended to do the same.

What the hell was I supposed to do?

"The lamb stew is supposed to be good here," the professor assured me after a moment.

"All right," I said. Did this board contain a list of the food they served here? That would make sense. "But it's too hot for stew. What else is good?" I didn't know about lamb—it was full summer and I doubted it would be fresh.

"They have a sirloin of beef, with horse radish," he told me, glancing down. "And a rabbit pot pie."

"That sounds good," I told him, hoping it wouldn't be too stringy. I set the stiff board to one side and looked up.

The professor was watching at me, careful like. "I could order for both of us," he said casually, though his eyes was still piercing.

"The rabbit," I told him. "With some carrots."

He glanced down at the board, but then jerked his head up at the shrill whistle of the armed coach.

A six-horse team came roaring down the street, scattering folks walking there, scaring a couple horses as well. It were armed with metal tubes along the sides that shot out rockets with some precision, or so I'd been told. Four stout men rode on the carriage, each standing on one corner of it, armed with pistols and rifles and who knew what else.

"My," the professor said after it had passed. "Does that contraption pass by at this time every day?"

"Near enough," I told him. "Locals know to stay out of the way," I assured him. It was loaded with payroll for the Broker's Mining Company, though I knew most of the money would go to the bosses and foremen and not the poor miners.

"That's good," the professor told me, using that smile that I still didn't know what to do with. Then he turned back to the stiff board he still help. "Maybe we should have some blackberry wine, as well?"

At least I knew my liquors. The blackberry wine they made around these parts was far too sweet. "Have you tried the spruce beer? It's a local drink." Or at least that's what the girls at the boarding house who'd come from other parts had told me.

"I've never even heard of spruce beer," he said, looking back up and smiling at me. He lifted his water glass, then raised it to me. "Here's to the start of what I hope is a great partnership."

"Partners," I told him, clinking glasses.

I couldn't tell him how much it thrilled me that he might even possibly consider me his equal.

How was I to know we'd soon be partners in crime?

Andrew came calling on me every day after that, and twice on Sunday, once in the morning to take me to church, then again in the afternoon, for a turn around the garden. We talked of all sorts of things, of gears and machines, of the new states being admitted to the Union, hell, even the suffragettes.

We didn't always agree, but at least he didn't mind me having an opinion. Encouraged me to speak my mind, even.

It was such a change after Mr. Dickerson's monologues on all things.

Mildred adored him, of course. "He's perfect for you!" she announced, coming into my room that first night after she'd met him. She scurried over and sat on my bed.

"Why so?" I asked. I actually wasn't sure. He sure was smart, and I liked that. And he liked that I was smart, too, and he wanted me to learn more about automatons.

But there was something that weren't sitting right with me. I couldn't put my finger on it.

"He's so smart! And such a gentleman. With such manners!" Mildred gushed.

I didn't snort at her, though I did ask her, "'Cause I'm so lady-like?"

"That's not what I mean," Mildred said. "You have a good heart, Grace," she added seriously.

I weren't sure about that. Mama hadn't really ever taught me to be good, or kind, even. For her, it had mostly been about fair. Sure, she might intimidate a customer, or confuse 'em, but she gave 'em good value and high quality moonshine for their two-bits.

"And he's so handsome, too," Mildred added. "You make a good-looking couple."

That I didn't doubt was true. I'd seen us in the window display downtown. With us both being so tall, and me standing up proud like Mama had taught me, I knew we'd turned heads.

However, that still didn't mean we should stay as we were.

"What about his stories, though?" I asked Mildred. "They change, sometimes."

If I was counting, he'd attended four different universities. Sometimes his parents had an inland farm in south Virginia, and other times they was close to the coast. And while he was good with automatronics, it was like the simplest things were beyond him.

He were smart, and kind. I knew that.

But I'd grown up with Mama. Somethin' weren't right with him.

"A man's always gonna tell you the stories he thinks you want to hear," Mildred told me. She held her hands over her lower belly, like she were protecting something there.

She'd sat like that before. Should I offer to make her a tonic or something to help her nerves? She'd never had a nervous stomach before.

Instead, I asked, "Now Mildred Peterson, where did you learn such a thing?" I was astonished at my little country mouse holding such an opinion.

She blushed hard and looked down at the floor, wringing her hands. "I don't know," she said.

I knew she was lying.

Then Mildred grew still. She spread her fingers wide across her severe black dress, pressing down on her thighs. After taking a deep breath she looked up, her washed out brown eyes boring into mine. "Does it really matter? That his stories change? Or that he looks at you with a calculating eye?"

I shifted uncomfortable on the bed. I hadn't realized that anyone but me saw that look.

But since Mildred had told me truthful, I had to tell her back. "It don't matter one bit."

He were here, in Hortonsville, only for a short time.

And when he were leaving, I'd set my mind to him taking me with.

That next Sunday, after church, I were waiting in my room for Andrew to come calling. His business in town was just about over, I knew. He'd mentioned an error in his hotel bill, which meant he were settling up.

I suspected that there weren't nothing in the bill, that he'd just weaseled out of paying for some of it.

And if he'd felt they'd owed him some money back, well, who was I to say he weren't right? He only wanted to pay what was fair.

He knew I believed in fair.

The summer was still coming on strong, heat like we didn't get in the hills. In my corner room I had two windows, with both open that afternoon in the empty hope of a breeze coming through. I sat at my desk, not drawing, not planning, not studying the schematics of nothing, just sitting.

I disgusted myself.

I should be able to make my own destiny. Go east, or west, or hell, all the way up north into Indian country.

But instead I sat, in my fancy dress, the sleeves confining my arms so I couldn't properly reach nothing, waiting for a man to get me out of my situation.

I was worse than Mama in a way—she couldn't help feeling blue sometimes.

I could do something. I just knew it.

I quickly added together all the bits of savings I had. I'd never put much into the banking account that Mr. Dickerson had opened for me—just never seemed right that I had to have him there to get at my own damn money. And he never learned about the other repair work I did, the trades I'd made.

Mama had always made sure I understood how important it was to get your cash from more than one place, and to store it in more than one locale, too. I was good with numbers, and I knew to the penny just how much money I could lay my hands on in less than an hour.

Then I considered the cost for those things I wanted, cursing myself for a fool.

I had enough for all the train tickets I'd need to get out to California, but not for the extras, like food, as well as the nights I'd have to spend in hotels along the way where the trip broke and the trains changed.

There weren't anything for me out there, either. I sure as hell weren't qualified to do some kind of clerking like Mildred. And I had no idea if repairing automatons was a job that traveled.

But I could always go back to moonshining if I needed to.

I made up my mind right then that even if Professor Andrew Sigler wouldn't take me along, I was going anyway.

I just had to figure out how to make up the coin for those last few things.

When one of the other girls came to fetch me, I'd composed myself again, no longer feverishly pacing like how Mama did when she'd get in a mood.

My gut hit my shoes, though, when I saw that Andrew had been at the boarding house for sometime, having coffee in the front sitting room with Mrs. Bailey. The curtains had all been drawn back, the sunlight showing off the fine velvet-and-wood couch and chairs, all done in shades of tan and brown. A thick red-and-gold oriental-style rug reflected back the light. It were a pain to beat and clean, and it sure were too fancy for my taste, but it set off the rest of the room nicely.

The good china sat on the carved, spindly end table—the white set of dishes with the delicate red strawberries painted on them that I was always afraid I'd crush accidental like. Mrs. Bailey still wore her good church dress. She looked like an actress in her brown silk dress with the high sleeves and the white buttons going from her wrists to her elbows, perfectly poised on the tan velvet chair.

"Gracie," Mrs. Bailey said, getting up slowly.

I held myself ready—seemed like she was gonna yell at me. Again. 'Twern't nothing I weren't used to.

"Why didn't you tell me your gentleman caller was such a delight?" she scolded.

"Ma'am, you'd have been telling me not to be bragging," I replied, pleased.

It weren't that I needed her approval none. I could make up my own damned mind about someone calling on me.

Still, it settled my heart some, knowing that he were good enough to fool her, too.

At least Mrs. Bailey weren't the simpering type. "I know you young people have things to say," she said. "Important things to talk about. I won't be standing in your way," she added, nodding her head to Andrew.

That set my back up. What was she talking about?

"You remind me of myself and my dear Mr. Bailey, god rest his soul. So in love," she added.

I didn't give her a laugh—she knew nothing about either of us. I don't think it was love, not really, not for either of us.

I'd deny to my grave how he sometimes made my stomach do that strange flip about.

"Shall we?" Andrew asked, holding out the crook of his arm again. He were dressed in that gray suit I liked so much, soft as dove feathers. I wore the dark green church dress that properly covered everything, though I'd done up my own corset—Mildred and the others always pulled it in too tightly, making it hard for me to breathe.

We walked out back, into the garden. The path was smooth brick, set wide enough so us girls could walk along it and not snag our skirts on any of the plants growing in the beds along it. Mrs. Bailey knew her roses, and how to keep 'em blooming through the summer. Took a lot of water, I knew. The whole garden was full of the heavy scent of 'em. She had herbs, too, though they was mostly for show and not for tinctures and tea. I coulda showed her, but she weren't interested.

Not a breeze blew down off the hills, and I was sweating even before we sat on the bench under the old oak on the far side of the garden, near the ivy-covered stone wall. Andrew was strangely quiet—I weren't sure what was going on in his head.

I'd set my mind to him taking me with him, though. Or somehow getting the money from him so I could go off on my own.

"Gracie, you know my business here is just about finished," he finally said, not looking at me but addressing his hands.

I'd never been completely sure of what exactly that business had been. "Have you enjoyed Hortonsville?" I asked him.

"The spruce beer was certainly lovely," he teased, glancing slyly up at me. Then he sighed and looked forward again.

I glanced over at him, cataloguing his profile: sharp nose; broad, intelligent forehead; bushy brown mustache; and clean-shaven cheeks. The only fault I could see in his character was a small chin, at odds with the rest of his profile, that some may have called weak.

But the intelligence in his eyes more than made up for that.

"Well, it certainly has been a treat, seeing you these last few weeks," I told him.

"Miss O'Malley, Gracie..." The professor hesitated, obviously not knowing where to start.

I let him dangle for a few moments before putting him out of his misery. "We've only just met, professor," I told him.

"But I feel as though I've known you forever," he said, leaping forward into the role I'd laid out for him. "As though our meeting was fated. You were meant to be there, in Mr. Dickerson's shop, to help me with the final design of my grand machine."

"That may be true, sir," I said. "And what would you have me do now?" I continued, laying it all out for him.

"Come with me, Gracie," the professor told me all in a rush. "We'll go to New York City. Then west."

"To California?" I asked. I won't lie, there may have been a bit of breathlessness in my voice.

"In the fanciest Pullman money can buy," he assured me.

Somehow, I knew he was lying.

And it didn't matter damned one bit.

"You know I can't just go with you," I told him. It were true. He needed to take that one last step.

Andrew looked up at me, alarmed.

I just smiled at him, waiting for him to get it.

"Oh!" he said. "I've been a fool." In one smooth motion, he slid around to one knee in front of me, taking my hand without asking.

Good thing I was feeling generous.

"Miss O'Malley, would you do me the honor of marrying me?" he asked.

I expected my stomach to do that damn flip again at those words, but it didn't. Instead, all I could see were the calculations in his eyes.

He was getting something, by me marrying him.

But Mama had always believed in fair. I was getting something too.

"Yes," I told him. "It'd be my honor."

The courthouse downtown was new, built out of blood-red bricks, with white pillars out front and a statue of a woman wearing a blindfold, holding a sword in one hand and a scale in the other, rising up above the twenty-foot-high wooden doors. Just inside the doors was an open and echoing hallway, making me feel like I'd just arrived from the hills. Two grand wooden staircases, one on either side of the room, curved up and met at the second floor.

We found the clerk's office downstairs. It weren't as fancy. A long wooden counter, like in Mr. Dickerson's shop, barred folks from the piles of papers and books sitting in the tall bookcases that filled the rest of the room. Long, thin windows set near the ceiling gave some light, but it was mostly dim and dark, even with the fancy, built-in gaslights.

"Can I help you?" An eager young man came forward. His white starched collar butted into his neck, and his vest were a faded black. His hands and hair looked soft. I'd bet he'd never worked a farm or even chopped his own wood.

"My sweetheart and I, well, we'd like to get married. Right away," Andrew said, his eyes sparkling.

I gave the clerk my best shy smile. At least, I'd tried.

Andrew passed the man a two-bit coin. "We're eloping," he said with a conspiratorial wink.

Which were kind of the truth. We'd not told no one. I didn't want the fuss, and Andrew seemed happy enough with that. I'd tell them all after, as I was saying goodbye.

The clerk showed more guts than I'd thought he'd have. "Ma'am?" he asked me. "Are you sure?"

"Yes, I want to marry this man," I assured the clerk. Andrew were my ticket out—if not all the way to California, at least to the next place along the way.

"We've known each other since we were ten years old," Andrew said, spinning easy lies. "Sweethearts since then," he added, squeezing my hand.

I'd suspected he were capable of it—it was nice to see proof. I merely nodded, giving my assent to his stories.

"But her father never cared for me, even after I made my fortune in automotronics. I still came back for my true heart," he said, giving me a smile that warmed those calculating eyes of his a little.

"And I agreed to go with him," I told the clerk. "Back to the city." I wasn't about to give away more of our plans.

Andrew smiled at me and patted my hand in approval.

Maybe we could have told the clerk the truth, but it just seemed easier this way.

I used my real name, though I knew I didn't have to. It was me getting married, so I wanted my name there. I even knew how to sign it and everything.

Andrew hesitated when the clerk asked him for the spelling of his name.

That was when I knew "Andrew Sigler" weren't the name his mama had given him.

But it were the name he'd used with me, the name I'd know him by. So that was who I married, Andrew Sigler, right there in the clerk's office by a judge, with the clerk and his friend witnessing the act.

We both took our vows before God, but really what mattered was in our hearts. We was promising to abide one another, at least for the time being.

I didn't know where Andrew got the ring—it weren't flashy like the advertisements Mildred had been showing me since she'd first met Andrew. It were solid metal, silver. When I looked closely, I could see two gears, interlocking, had been etched on the side.

That Andrew had given me something like that meant more to me than any of the flowers or dinners or suppers or walks we'd ever taken.

When the deed was done, we walked back out into the bright sunshine. I felt a bit breathless, like we'd just climbed some great hill and was about to step off, with no bridge there below us.

"Well, Mrs. Sigler, what would you like to do for the afternoon?" he asked, patting my hand and tucking it into his elbow.

"Let's go to the Windgate room, and have the fanciest champagne supper they have," I suggested. I'd never been there either, and I knew we couldn't afford it.

I didn't care none. I was married—something I weren't sure would ever have happened to me.

"Perfect!" Andrew said, smiling at me. "Then we should pack," he said seriously. "We'll head out on the seven-ten in the morning, make it to New York City by nightfall."

"You were serious about that?" I asked, surprised. I knew he'd been lying about something he'd said about his plans.

"We may have to stay in New York for a bit," he amended. "But I've had California in my sights for some time now."

"What do you plan on doing out there?" I asked, walking down the broad walk and not paying no mind to another soul. I were a properly married woman, now.

"I'm sure there's a market for my marvelous automatronics," he said breezily.

"I could help run your store," I said shyly. "Keep all the accounts in my head."

"I was counting on that," he said warmly, patting my hand. "You're a marvel with numbers. And with my inventions, as well."

Damn, there came that same feeling he always gave me.

The waiters at the Windgate were happy to let us sit by the window, as Andrew insisted.

It were his habit. Wherever we went for lunch, he was always insisting we look out on the street. He'd watch the people, but mainly he'd watch the carriages and automatons going by.

And the armed coaches.

We had a sparkling dinner none-the-less, with fresh caught trout and champagne, toasting each other and confessing our recent wedding to everyone sitting nearby.

The only time Andrew got quiet was when the noon coach rolled down the street, his calculating eyes taking in the horses' gait, the number of men, their arms and condition.

I didn't say nothing, of course.

I insisted on going back to Mrs. Bailey's rooms that afternoon and packing up by myself.

"I'll buy you all new dresses in New York City," Andrew assured me. "And new boots as well."

"There's other things I want, there," I told him. "My tools and drawings." Which was true. "I'll be back with you in an hour," I promised him as I hurried off.

Maybe Andrew would buy me all new dresses, but maybe he wouldn't. There still were something going on with him. I doubted our wedding had left him so breathless as me.

Mama had taught me to keep my armament clean, and to always check my own damn gun. I figured my dresses were the least of what I needed packing, besides my tools and gears and everything else I'd saved away under the boards of the floor and the false back I'd built into my wardrobe.

That timid knock came on the door while I was still packing. I opened the door myself, grateful it was who I was expecting—a tearful Mildred.

"Come in," I said, pulling her inside quickly. I didn't have a lot of time. Andrew would be picking me up soon and I had to finish gathering together all my things.

"I'm so happy for you," Mildred gulped through her tears. "I really am. I just—Grace O'Malley, what is that?"

I turned and showed her the gun. "Gift from Mama," I told her truthfully.

"Now why in the world would you be packing that along?" she asked, shocked as I put it in the trunk with everything else.

"Wouldn't do to leave it here and have the next girl find it, right?" I asked her.

"What did you—I had no idea this was here!" Mildred said as she looked at the back of my wardrobe and saw the door.

"You weren't supposed to," I told her. "But maybe, if you can, you could arrange to take my room after I'm gone." Mildred hadn't been here as long as some of the other girls, so she didn't have seniority. But she did have a family who'd be willing to pay more money.

"I don't think I'll be here for long," she said. She folded her hands across her stomach, as had become her habit of late.

What were going on with her?

"But you been practicing, I know it!" I told her. "You're getting better at the typing machines." I didn't think they was going to fire her or something.

"I can type just fine, now," Mildred admitted. "But Mr. Lawson, he's been coming by my desk, almost every afternoon."

"You sly one," I told Mildred. "You gonna hook yourself a husband, too?"

Mildred looked down at her hands, but they was still. "Maybe," she said. "But you listen here, Grace O'Malley. Don't you believe all the things any man tells you."

I stopped my packing and came over to my friend—probably the only friend I'd ever had. "I know that," I told her. I took her hands in mine, surprised at how warm they was. "I've known that for a lot longer than you have," I told her honestly. "Everybody be lying about something," I added. "You just have to figure out what's an okay lie." What would be fair.

"That's not what the bible says, but you may be right." Mildred shook her head, then straightened up. "You go ahead and find God's light in your life," she said firmly. "It will help you chose the right lie."

"Sounds like you're finding your strength," I told her.

She smiled at me. "Growing into our names," she said proudly. "Now, what else do you have hidden here that I should know about?"

I'd just finished showing her all the hiding spaces in the room when a knock came on the door.

It were Mrs. Bailey herself.

"You know, I've always been proud of you," she said, holding herself tall, though she'd never be able to look me in the eye. "You've grown so much from that wild woods girl. Now look at you!"

I glanced around. I had a dear friend I was leaving, who was probably in some kind of trouble, and two trunks worth of goods.

I'd come down with a bag and the clothes on my back.

I could leave it all behind, though, if I had to. The things I'd packed didn't matter none.

What mattered was that I was leaving.

I gave Mildred a long teary hug, shook hands with Mrs. Bailey, then left with my head held high.

I was finally moving on.

The next morning people on the train station platform was buzzing with news. There was papers, but I couldn't read them none. Andrew said it weren't nothing, just some ruffians and a brawl downtown, late last night.

While we was having our wedding nuptials.

Fortunately, I wasn't the blushing kind.

But Andrew had made me appreciate why Mama sometimes got wild when she came into town.

It weren't until Andrew had gone off with a porter to arrange for our luggage to be properly stored that I learned the truth.

Seemed one of the armed coaches had been held up. The guards had been blinded by some kind of lighted flying machines. The robbers had been aided by a mechanical cart, about the size of a card table, that had appeared out of nowhere on the train tracks beside the coach.

I watched Andrew give the porter a healthy tip. He weren't fussing about money that morning. Seems his accounts was all flush again.

He'd been fairly paid for his work, and now it was time to move to another town, find a new job.

Something that I might help with as well.

Married or not, we was partners.

And he had broke me out.

This is the first Gracie story that I wrote. It was written for the anthology, "Clockwork Universe." It was also the first steampunk/wild west story that I'd ever written.

By the time I finished, I knew I had to write more Gracie stories. There was so much about her and her world that I wanted to explore.

GRACIE'S FIRE

Other-of-a-whore my boots hurt. They pinched my toes, chafed my ankles, and the damn heels made my back and calves ache. The best part of every night was finally getting home to the garret above the feed shop and taking 'em off. Even if they was a present from my long-lost husband, god bless his soul, made outta solid black leather with brass hooks and laces, they felt like they was taking orders from the devil himself.

I still wore 'em with a smile. I even practiced walking as gracefully as I could, from one end of The Gold Mine Saloon to the other, across the sawdust and straw-strewn floor, balancing my tray with one hand, like they did at the Barstow Hotel, in the fancy part of town. They did make my hips sway, which garnered attention and more tips. Tips that

I saved, tips that were gonna get me out of that garret and maybe buy me my own piece of land someday.

Not that I was likely to get any tips tonight. The saloon was deader than a priest's cell on a Saturday night. The seven-twenty train from Sacramento wasn't coming in: bridge had flooded out (again). As we was directly across the muddy street from the train station, it brought us most of our trade.

As for folks from here in Stockton, well, Lucky Lucy's had just opened down the street—and they had dancing girls.

Mister Thomas didn't much approve of them. He didn't make us strip down to nothing either. I couldn't have worn my dress to church, but it only bared my shoulders, ankles, and arms. I kinda liked the color too, a rich gold across my chest that didn't show the dirt too much, over a black short-sleeved blouse and a hitched up skirt. It showed off that pale Irish skin of mine, and Mister Thomas said the gold matched my green eyes. Nothing worked with my hair of course—I wore it shamefully short, and it was too thick and black to be much use.

The only "special" that The Gold Mine Saloon had to offer was that hulking steam-powered contraption that took up half the bar, another one of Mister Thomas' inventions. Me and the girls done made him get rid of most of thems: the weird, flickering, automatic lights (we all preferred gaslight); the odd moving belt for taking the dishes back to the kitchen (it was nice of him to try and save us some steps, but the pile ups and broken glassware made all our lives hell); and the clockwork automaton that used to run the drink machine (Mister Thomas said it wasn't alive, and its eyes was just glass, but it'd still watch all the girls walk around the saloon, giving us chills).

We had traditional kegs of beer, bottles of cheap whisky, and cheap moonshine—cloudy liquid in big bottles that'd eat anything, even brass, if we tried cleaning with it. I coulda made better, but Mister Tomas didn't want to get into the distilling business, not like that.

However, the machine, well, it could make pretty much any drink. Large glass jars of colored liquid—pink, brown, green, blue, and yellow—stuck out of one end of the sleek brass, like a peacock's tail. At least a dozen knobs, wheels, and gears regulated the flow and temperature of the liquid as it churned through the machine. The twisting spigot on the other end looked like glass, but it was hard as diamond.

That contraption could make damn near anything. Fizzy, sparkling lemonade that tasted like the perfect summer day. Dark, rich wine that reminded you of Mama's stews in deep winter. That odd, blue drink that left smoke on your tongue and tears in your eyes.

A lot of the locals didn't care much for the machine, never buying drinks from it. But sometimes a riverboat hand or a farmer'd get drunk, tell me to make 'em whatever I felt like.

I always got a good tip from that.

Sometimes stupid cowpokes would come in, drunk already, then dare each other to come up with wilder concoctions, and force 'em down.

Then I'd have to shove 'em out the door before they started puking.

Tonight, though, no one was ordering nothing. Mister Thomas was at his regular weekly poker game—the one I'd rescued him from at least twice over the years—and had left me in charge for the night, as usual. Old Dusky sat at the bar, nursing his customary one whisky. He were a regular, but rarely talked. Just sat, had his one drink, drawing patterns on the bar with his finger. Two businessmen sat in one corner, talking about some land deal they was putting together.

And that was it.

I'd already sent all the other girls home, so it was just me behind the long bar. Me in those damn boots that I daydreamed about burning in the grate at the far end of the saloon. I'd set my mind to close the bar early—kick Dusky out and start moving the businessmen along—when the doors swung open and in came this group of four men.

Well, at first I thought they was men. They was in these big black cloaks with the hoods up, shapeless and hiding their faces. But they were regular height, and didn't look too wide, either.

"Gentlemen," I called out. "We're clos—"

That's when I realized something was wrong.

They turned to stare at me, all of 'em together, like they was one person, really. Peeking out from underneath those black hoods was some of the orangest skin I'd ever seen, like they was pumpkins or something. They had weird black eyes and no real noses. Their lips were thin and chins were long and pointed, with warts, like what a witch would wear.

Course I didn't scream or nothing. Didn't know what they were, had never seen nothing like them before, but they was obviously from out of town.

Wouldn't know real prices for anything, and it weren't like we had anything written down, even if they could read.

And maybe they'd be good tippers, besides.

I got 'em settled at a table in the center of the saloon. I cut Dusky off, sent him along his way. The businessmen didn't look too happy about the outsiders there, so it weren't too long before they was gone too.

Which left just me and the four newcomers.

"So what'll it be, boys?" I asked, coming out from behind the bar, letting my hips sway just a bit.

None of them paid any attention. They all looked me directly in the face.

That'd never happened before.

"Whissskey," said the first guy. He was a little taller than the others.

I couldn't really read his expression, but he seemed proud of himself.

"Whisky all around?" I asked. They didn't nod, but they didn't disagree either. "I'll bring a bottle. That'll be a quarter eagle." I wasn't about to bring nobody no booze without payment first. At their blank looks, I added "Two-fifty."

It was only two bits more than the regular price. I was just including my tip in the cost.

They had some kind of hissing language they used with each other. Sounded like drunk Mexican to me. The tall one brought out a gold piece from his sleeve and slid it across the table.

I didn't try to count how many fingers he had—as long as he kept them to himself, we was gonna be just fine.

He'd passed me a full eagle—ten whole dollars. "I'll keep this as your tab," I told him, picking up the coin and weighing it. Didn't bother tasting it until after I'd turned away, but it was pure gold as far as I could tell.

I wouldn't have kept the whole thing, if they hadn't spent it all by the end of the evening. I would have given them change. Or at least some of it. My mama may not have been kind, but she did raise me to be fair. Mostly.

I brought 'em back a bottle of the cheapest stuff we had, along with four clean glasses. Then I went back behind the bar, cleaned up Dusky's glass, the businessmen's, and watched my new guests.

They didn't seem quite sure what to do at first. Eventually, they figured it out, pouring the booze into the glasses, then the glasses down their throats.

Maybe they weren't complete strangers, because they swallowed down stuff that would strip the finish off the bar and didn't cough or sputter once.

After they'd finished off a third of the bottle, they seemed to loosen up, as all men do. They leaned back in their chairs, and the tall one even flipped his hood back.

Damn, he was ugly. Bald as a baby's butt, with a dark web of lines growing like tree roots out of the back of his neck and up into his skull. His black eyes shone wet and long, kind of like a horse's. He hissed at the others, getting them to flip their hoods back too.

The others were just as ugly, though I'd been right—Big Baldy was the tallest of the group, and had the strongest features. The others were smaller, not like kids, but not fully grown, either.

I couldn't make heads or tails outta their hissing talk. They did seem worried about something. I sure hoped it wasn't the money, that they weren't thinking about robbing the place. I couldn't get the day's take out of the bar and to the bank until morning.

While they was pouring another round for themselves, I got the revolver Mister Thomas had given me, that I'd taught all the other girls to use. It weren't one of his inventions, no, it was a real Smith and Wesson, a six-shooter, that I made damn sure was kept cleaner than brand new sheets from the Sears and Roebuck Catalog.

I also started up the coals under the big kettle, so I'd have plenty of steam later if I needed it. Mister Thomas didn't approve of us wasting his special coal and heating up the water before a client asked for a drink from the machine, but I had a feeling about these four.

Once Big Baldy and the others had finished their whisky, I came out from behind the bar again. "Want another?" I asked. They was all leaning way back in their chairs now, loose in the way a cowpoke gets after a hard night's whoring.

"Thisss machine," Big Baldy said, waving his hand toward the beast on the bar. "How much for it?"

"Y'all got enough on your tab for more drinks," I told him. "Anything special you want? Or should I just make you something?"

"Make ussss, yessss, make usss ssssomething." Big Baldy pressed his thin lips together, tightly, pushing them outward.

Hell, was that a smile? Or was he making a kissy face at me?

I sure didn't stick around to find out. I went back behind the bar, tightened the ends of the hoses connected to the kettle, then opened up the valves so the steam would rise, powering the machine.

It came to life slowly, despite the head of steam I'd already built up. The bottles gurgled—the blue one especially—as seals formed, making sure nothing leaked. Then the dials started lighting up, one after another, showing temperature, pressure, moisture, and a bunch of things Mister Thomas had told me that I didn't remember and couldn't read, having never learned my letters.

So what would it be for Big Baldy? I paused in my considering, looking over the machine at him. He still leaned back, like a lazy cat, playing with the glass in front of him.

What would make him relax more? I remembered thinking about whoring. Maybe that was what this crew needed. Something that would both relax 'em, and raise 'em up.

I started with the yellow—liquid gold, as Mister Thomas likened it. Then some brown: Those boys needed some earthiness. A touch of blue for whimsy. Then topped it off with the pink, for the frills of the dancing girls up the street.

It didn't take the machine long to process, huffing and puffing as it blended the liquids in its sleek innards, finally distilling the prettiest orange drink at the other end.

I was congratulating myself as I took the first glass over. It looked a perfect match. I was sure to get a big tip from this.

But Big Baldy looked askance at it. "What isss thisss?"

"You asked me to make you something," I shot back.

Mister Thomas would be so mad at me if I wasted a drink from the machine. He sometimes got angry enough to take it out of my wages. I always made it back, though, fixing something that broke either at the bar or in town.

"Ssssomething humansss, yessss," Big Baldy replied.

Human? Well, hell. These boys really weren't from around these parts.

Not like I was gonna stop making 'em drinks, though. We even served Indians here at the Gold Mine Saloon.

"Tis human," I told him. "I made it from the machine built by Mister Thomas. You should try it," I coaxed. "Just a sip. I'm sure it's good for what ails you."

Big Baldy glared at me, glared at the glass I offered him, but he finally reached out with those too-many fingers and took the drink.

He brought it to his nose—no idea if he could smell anything through those tiny slits. I was afraid he was gonna unfurl a tongue or something to taste it first, but he brought it to his mouth, taking a small sip.

After Big Baldy smacked his lips together like an old timer who'd lost all his teeth, he finally looked back up at me. "Issss good!"

"One for each?" I asked, nodding at the other gents.

"Yessss! One for everyone here! You too!" Big Baldy said expansively. "Tell usssss your name?"

"Gracie," I told him. It wouldn't harm none, and might keep 'em friendlier, later.

'Cause I could see that keeping 'em friendly now weren't gonna be a problem—that drink had turned Big Baldy into one jovial pumpkin.

☆

"Now boys, I'm sorry to tell you, but it's closing time," I eventually told Big Baldy and his friends, Frick, Frack, and Nod. I had no idea what any of their names were, but I was plum tired, through and through.

And my feet were *still* killing me.

They'd tossed me an extra eagle, for my troubles. But it weren't enough to keep me going, not when dawn was creeping up outa the east.

"Gracccie," Big Baldy sang out. "Jusssst one more. Pleasssssse?"

I'd already planned on that. "Last call," I said. "Last one. Then, vamoose."

Big Baldy actually giggled at that, like a weird pumpkin child. "Vamooooshhhh!" he said, his hand flying through the air, toward Frick, Frack, and Nod.

They chittered at that, like not quite full-grown giggles.

I knew what I should make them to get them moving along—a drink of home.

It was a gamble. It might make 'em morose. I'd done that once already, mixing 'em a drink with too much of the yellow and not enough brown.

But they still needed to be moseying along.

So I gave them great brown muddy skies, with dots of yellow stars, blue hard rocks and soft pink nests.

Then I mixed up something for me. Started with a solid moonshine base, then mixed in a dash of all the colored liquids.

Mister Thomas had told me once never to add everything in. It would muddy the drink. Too much of everything and not enough of a single taste, a single feeling.

But I wasn't so tired that I couldn't coax that machine to sit up and sing for its supper if I set my mind to it.

The drinks for Big Baldy were all a muddy brown, while mine was the color of fire, red and furious.

I'd actually made this drink one time before, named it after myself: Gracie's Fire.

I merely sipped my cordial, planning to finish it later, while the boys slammed theirs back, as I thought they might. "So it's a good evening to ya," I said as I came back out from behind the bar, tray in hand. I collected their glasses and the empty bottle, then turned back toward the bar.

Big Baldy and the others hissed at each other. I had no idea what language it was, but they sounded more intent now, not so relaxed.

I got myself back behind the bar again, brought the revolver up beside me, and waited.

"Gracccccie," Big Baldy said, standing, swaying.

I took a sip of my own drink, "It's been fun, gentlemen, but I gotta close up, and you have to go."

"Not without you, Gracccie," Big Baldy said.

He made that kissy face again. Shit, he was ugly.

"And your marvelousssss masssssshine."

Damn it. I knew they was gonna be trouble sooner or later.

I picked up the revolver and cocked it. "Can't have it. Need y'all to just move along, now."

"Gracccccie, you wouldn't sssssshoot usssss," Big Baldy said confidently.

I put a bullet into the floor, directly in front of his feet.

Mama may not have been the best, but she made sure I was well-versed in the essentials: Shooting and moonshine.

Mister Thomas would just have to understand about the hole in the floor.

Big Baldy started, then stood up straight. The others chittered at him. He raised one of his odd, too-many-fingered hands and silenced them.

"I got five bullets still warm and waiting," I told him. "Now, you've been good customers, so let's just leave it at that."

Big Baldy shook his head. "I'm sssssssorry, Gracccccie." He held up some kind of weapon of his own. It looked like a short rifle, but the end was blown out, like a trumpeter's horn.

Now, I'd seen duels out on the street. No one was ever a winner. And while I was fast, I couldn't take down four of them, not before I got myself shot.

I was just gonna have to sweet talk my way out of this. Unfortunately, being sweet wasn't something Mama had ever bothered to teach me.

I kept the gun pointed directly at Big Baldy's chest, while with my other hand I took a sip of my drink. Casual like. Not because I needed the extra courage. Or to prove to myself that I could do this without my hand shaking.

It warmed me from tip to toes, like the sun was already coming up and heating me up on the inside. "Now, gentlemen," I said. "Let's be reasonable about this. I'm sure we can work something out."

Before I could say another word, Big Baldy shook his head. "No," he said.

Then he shot me.

You know those old houses, out on the prairie, that get abandoned after the fever runs through, or maybe the Indians come in and kill everyone? The way the walls all crumble in, bricks and boards collapsing to dust?

That was how my bones felt. Big Baldy's gun shot out a huge black net that wrapped around my chest, pinning my arms to my sides and making my bones feel like they was all crumbly, nothing solid left inside.

Luckily, I was able to stay upright. Damn boots hurt too much for me to lose feeling with my feet: They was strapped in too tight to turn to dust like the rest of my bones.

Frick, Frack, and Nod all swarmed up over the bar. They made hissing noises at the machine, stroking it and chittering.

Big Baldy looked all too pleased with himself.

But they hadn't pinned my arms all the way, just across my shoulders and my chest. I still had my hands free.

They wasn't paying me no mind.

I didn't have my gun anymore. I'd dropped that when I'd been hit.

But I could still reach my drink.

It was mostly colored moonshine, something these idiots had no idea about.

Mister Thomas could always replace the bar. But he couldn't replace the machine. He'd told me that himself.

With careful, slow movements, I reached for my glass. My hands were shakier than the legs on a newborn calf. I had to watch my fingers to make sure they closed, then tightened, around the drink.

Just as slowly, I brought my hand up and my mouth down, getting a good mouthful of the liquid.

Gracie's Fire.

I didn't swallow it down, though it burned. I took small breaths, afraid the fumes would knock me out.

I took one stumbling step, then another, before I finally reached the lamp on the edge of the bar.

"Gracccccie, where are you going?" Big Baldy asked. He sounded like he was laughing.

That just made me push my poor, abused feet forward one more step. Then another.

I stumbled around the end of the bar until the lamp stood between me and Big Baldy, then clumsily knocked the lamp off, exposing the flame.

"I won't hurtsssss you," Big Baldy assured me.

With my mouth full, I couldn't tell him, *Too bad. Cause I'm about to hurt you.*

Then I blew that pure moonshine straight onto the flame.

An arc of fire jumped from the light and hit Baldy straight in the chest.

Big Baldy fell back on his ass, screaming, his cloak flaming up nicely. He beat at the flames with both hands, not paying me any mind.

Frick, Frack, and Nod took one look at him, and skedaddled.

Seemed they didn't feel like being toasted.

As best I could, I stripped off that damn net. It was sticky and clung to my fingers like spiderwebs. But I peeled it off and dove for my gun, finally holding it with still weak hands, pointing it right at Big Baldy's chest as he rose up from the ground.

The gun he'd used on me was out of his reach, still on the bar. I picked it up too, pointing it straight at his head. "Keeping this as collateral," I told him. "Now git." I started walking toward him.

Big Baldy's cloak was in tatters. Seemed he was just as orange all over, with weird black lines pulsing over his skin, like a map of a river delta.

"We needsssss the massssshine," Big Baldy complained as he started backing toward the door.

"Then come during business hours and make a deal with Mister Thomas," I told him.

When Baldy stopped moving, I put another bullet in the floor. "Git."

"We will return," he warned, but he left.

I locked the doors behind him and leaned back, taking a deep breath.

I had no doubt they'd come back. But I also had faith in Mister Thomas. Once he'd taken apart that gun they'd left behind, he'd know exactly what kind of drink I should serve 'em next time.

I took another sip of Gracie's Fire, thanking Mama for having raised me right, with a steady hand and a solid appreciation of moonshine.

After I made sure that Frick, Frack, and Nod hadn't broken that damn contraption, I could finally close up the saloon for the night, head back up to my garret.

And take my damn boots off.

Chronologically speaking, there are actually several stories that occur between "Gracie's Fire" and "Gracie and the Gold Mine." Like when Andrew comes back from the dead. And Gracie meeting the storm tamer. And the times she's saved Mr. Thomas. And...You get the idea.

There will be many more Gracie stories to come.

GRACIE AND THE GOLD MINE

You bought a what?" I asked Mister Thomas.

I may have set my shot glass down more forceful than I shoulda—the loud thunk ricocheted through the empty barroom of the Gold Mine Saloon. All the parts of the disassembled revolver laying across the wood bar jumped and rattled.

At least there weren't any liquor left in the glass. Mama woulda scolded me fierce for being disrespectful of the drink.

"No, Gracie, not bought," Mister Thomas told me. "I won. Well. Acquired. A gold mine. Up in the Sierra Nevada foothills."

He fiddled with his cufflinks, straightened his ascot tie, and didn't look at me direct-like.

"It's still rich in gold. It just needs to be flushed out," he added.

I knew something shady had gone on. I just hoped I wouldn't have to clean it up later, like I usually did.

"And how do you aim to do that?" I said, still trying to imagine Mister Thomas out in the wild. It weren't that he didn't know how to use his hands—he weren't a completely soft fool—but he weren't from the country neither. He grew up reading and writing, waited on by servants, not chopping wood and making do on his own. "You got a new automaton planned, don't you?"

"I might, I might at that," Mister Thomas said, finally looking up and smiling at me. He did have a nice smile that genuinely reached his brown eyes. A boyish smile, some mighta called it, though I knowed he were in his late twenties, about the same age as me. "And that's why I want you to come with me. To the mine."

Of course he wanted me with him. And it weren't because he wanted no woman's comfort in bed: He was my employer—he owned the Gold Mine Saloon—and was very proper. He kept his eyes on my face and my green eyes and not on my hips, no matter how I walked around the bar waiting on folks. I never even caught him looking at my neck, though I wore my coarse black hair shamefully short, and the black and gold dress I had for the bar showed off my collarbone and my white Irish skin.

I'd give Mister Thomas credit though: He was smart enough to know he needed someone practical around, someone who could take care of his camp up in the hills and see that he got food in him when his head was off in the clouds. He knew I could shoot and trap, too.

"I don't know nothing about mining," I warned him. "And I sure don't know about inventing a whole new whirligig."

While I was good at fixing automatons, I weren't no inventor, not like him.

"Gracie O'Malley," Mister Thomas said as he settled himself down on a stool across the bar from me. "You don't give yourself enough credit."

Now, while I never been raised by Mama to be ladylike, I still knowed better than to snort at him. Just told him, "I don't think so. I'm happy here in Stockton," as I went back to polishing the revolver I kept behind the bar.

Mama had always told me to keep my gun clean and my shot dry. Though the six-shooter used cartridges, not powder, I still followed her advice.

The bar weren't open yet, but the round tables was all set up (about half a dozen) with cheap chairs set round, and a righteous amount of sawdust spilled across the wooden floor, good for catching spit, spilled drinks and the occasionally drop of blood.

Not like we'd be having much business even if we was open. Between Lucky Lucy's up the street and The Golden Corral that had just opened on the other side, our trade was drying up.

Course, they had dancing girls, something Mister Thomas didn't approve of.

All we had was the big steam-powered machine sitting on the bar, another of Mister Thomas' inventions. One end of it bristled with brightly colored bottles, like a giant mechanical peacock. It had a long brass body full of dials and switches, then out the other end come every kind of drink you could imagine—and plenty you couldn't. Like the milky-colored shots Old Pedro liked that reminded him of fermented cactus milk, or the fire and smoke I coaxed out of it that tasted like one of Mama's herbal infusions of moonshine that cured all of what ailed you.

"So what do you say?" Mister Thomas asked.

I told him, "No," checking the alignment of the barrel on the six-shooter, not meeting his eye. I could play this game too.

"I'll tell you what, then," Mister Thomas said. "I'll pay you a quarter eagle per day, plus fifty percent of the gold."

Now, I did give him a snort. "I don't think so," I told him.

There was something fishy about how Mister Thomas acquired this gold mine of his. For all his smarts, he weren't that bright sometimes. There was no saying if any of the gold what come out would be his or not, or if he'd lose it in some foolish bet, like he had before.

"Half eagle per day, and thirty percent," I said.

I also weren't about to bet against him.

"Splendid! Done!" Mister Thomas said. "Let us drink to our new partnership."

I didn't recall no talk about being partners, and I was pretty sure when I did find out, I weren't gonna like it.

Still, I weren't about to back out.

Mister Thomas slipped off his stool and came around to the business side of the bar, stepping up to his machine.

What come out looked like liquid gold, heavy and rich as cream, but it sparkled on my tongue like spring sunshine.

"So what kind of machine you got in mind to get that gold out of them hills?" I finally asked him.

"It won't just be automatons, Gracie," Mister Thomas confided, leaning closer. "I'll be using something else as well. Alchemy."

I'd never heard of no alchemy before. It sounded like some kind of dark magic, like the folks who would make the sign of the evil eye to turn away Mama's gaze. Not that she were evil, just touched.

I just nodded, though, smart-like, 'cause I knew Mister Thomas couldn't help but tell me about it.

However, he surprised me that night. "I'll get out of your way now, let you open up. Inform the girls we'll be closing up for a week, starting next Monday, while we go off to make our fortune."

"What ain't you telling me?" I finally asked Mister Thomas.

"It'll be a trick getting there," he admitted. "And getting the gold out. But we'll manage, old girl." And with that, Mister Thomas walked to the door and opened it, indicating that we was open for business and I didn't have another chance to ask him questions.

Even if I'd knowed then what I know now, how I'd feel at the end of this, I still woulda gone.

I took one look at Mister Thomas' airship floating back behind his house, tied to what looked like a fancy metal hitching post, and I put my bag right down.

"No," I told him. "No way in hell am I traveling anywhere in that."

I was already sweating in the heavy winter coat Mister Thomas had insisted I wear for this trip. Now, I had chills all up and down my spine as well.

I'd seen a couple of those nice air balloons, all colorful and sailing, well, *gracefully* through the air. And an airship too, bullet-shaped as it swam through the clouds.

This weren't nothing like those.

The balloon part weren't sleek: It had odd bulges, like fish fins, one up top, to the right, and one on the bottom, to the left, but not directly opposite. It were made out of brown canvas, dirty and patched. The engines at the back were all I recognized as Mister Thomas' work: They had that same clean feeling of most of his automatons. The blades curved nicely, and the steam-tubes feeding them flowed pretty around the bulk of the machinery.

"It's perfectly safe," Mister Thomas assured me, coming out from the shed in the back of his yard. He wore a long brown coat, streaked with oil and dirt, to protect his nicer clothes underneath. Big-eyed goggles pushed back his curly brown hair, showing his broad forehead and making him look younger than ever.

Of course he would say that. The airship looked dinged up, nothing new, only the engines put together right. But there was something off with them as well.

"God meant us to fly, he woulda give us wings," I said. Then I clamped my lips together tightly. I sounded like that slope-eyed reverend I'd knowed growing up. I'd hated that man, still blamed him for Mama's death.

I didn't take my words back, though. That ship filled me with a fright.

"You've ridden on trains, though, right Gracie?" Mister Thomas asked, all gentle-like. "And God didn't give us wheels."

I had to nod. He had a point.

"Why do you want to ride in this thing and not on mules like civilized folks?" I had to ask. I wasn't giving in, not yet. But I was curious. It weren't just for fun, or rather, Mister Thomas' idea of fun, was it?

"Going there straight as the crow flies will get us there quicker," Mister Thomas told me. "In hours instead of weeks. And, well, that's always been the issue. There's no road to the site."

"What do you mean?" I asked. I knowed there were problems with this mine.

"There's a road to the camps on either side," Mister Thomas assured me. "But those roads belong to those miners.

All I acquired were the rights to the mine. Not the right to use the neighbor's roads."

"So you got you a mine you can't get to?" I asked. Sounded just like the type of fool thing Mister Thomas would do.

"Yes," Mister Thomas said, chuckling. "The gentleman who gave it to me thought it would be useless. But he really didn't want it to fall into either of his neighbor's hands." Mister Thomas gave me that boyish smile of his, the ones that made his eyes twinkle. "He didn't realize I was an inventor."

No, just figured you were some other type of idjit. But I didn't say nothing.

Mister Thomas had no idea the type of feud we might be sailing into. I knew of blood feuds up in the hills where I'd growed up lasting for generations.

I left my bag where it was and started walking around the whirligig. Those engines was still bothering me. Finally figured out that only one was in place to power the ship, almost directly behind it, though a little to the left. The other was off kilter, up on the right, and it weren't connected up proper.

"Why two engines?" I asked Mister Thomas. Was the other a spare?

"To carry away all the gold!" Mister Thomas told me cheerfully.

I sighed and shook my head. While we might need that extra power with a heavier load, we might also need it before then, if the one good engine give out.

Or was shot out.

I was gonna have to modify that right quick. At least connect it up.

"You sure this is the only way?" I asked, resigned to this foolishness.

"Yes. You'll love it!" Mister Thomas promised.

I was more afraid that he might be right than that he might be wrong.

I never thought I'd be flying through the air, up above the fields and towns this way. It done took my breath away to be so far up, to see so clearly all around us. The blue sky looked clear and cold, and that was what it was, not as warm as down closer to the earth that could hold the sunshine. The ground below was a patchwork quilt of browns and greens, cut up by roads and fields.

The cabin we stood in was just a big box of plain wood, attached to the airship by ropes cinched up with gears in the four corners. The front of the cabin held one big glass window, with two small round ones on the sides. It weren't warm in that cabin: I was glad I'd listened to Mister Thomas and worn my heaviest coat and gloves.

Attached to its own stand was something Mister Thomas called a *dashboard*. It was obviously his own invention, the dials ordered and gauges set out precise and in a pleasing order. Mister Thomas used a large wooden ship's wheel to steer the rudder, in the back of the ship.

One of Mister Thomas' automatons, the silver manlike thing he'd tried to have in the bar serving drinks, was shoveling the coal to the engine. Not normal stuff, no, but Mister Thomas' special blend, lighter than normal coal, more condensed so we needed less.

"Quite a sight, isn't it, Gracie old girl," Mister Thomas said. I knowed he wanted to say it gentle-like, he had that look about him. He felt the same wonder I did.

But with the wind blowing and the roar of the engine, he had to shout, same as me. I just nodded. The view made my heart beat funny and my breath catch. I'd never been in love. Maybe this was something like that, though. For the first time, I wished Mama was still alive, that she could have seen something like this.

Course it couldn't last.

Tremors started under my palm where I held onto the cabin, growing steady. I didn't even have to ask Mister Thomas what was wrong: His face showed a mighty worry.

"The wind's starting early," Mister Thomas told me. He flipped a lever. The sound of hissing—like gas escaping—filled the cabin.

We started to go down.

"Are we gonna crash?" I asked. Figured I should prepare myself now.

"No," Mister Thomas said, but his mouth was just a line, no smile now. "Hang on!"

The carriage of the airship started to swing up. I braced my feet and hung onto the dashboard.

"We just have to do some tacking," Mister Thomas explained. "Like a sailboat. Until the worst of the winds die down."

The odd fins suddenly made sense. Even a tall boat sailing into harbor couldn't come in directly if the wind was blowing out. It had to tack back and forth. Smaller boats went up on one edge doing this.

That was also why the second engine was off center, up on the side instead of directly behind the airship, to give extra weight to swing the ship up.

The airship gained speed as we tacked against the wind. It were odd, sailing so fast through the air at this angle. Mountains full of deadly rocks first threatened us from the left side, then we come about, and they were on our right.

"What's the site look like? What's the landmark?" I asked.

"Look for a rock like an old timer, with a big nose," Mister Thomas told me.

Weren't hard to spot the bare rock: It looked like a blind man with his nose broke more than once. "There!" I told Mister Thomas, pointing.

Mister Thomas tacked that way gracefully. He pulled on a lever on his right, frowned, then pulled harder.

But we wasn't slowing down any.

"I believe we may have a bit of a problem," Mister Thomas said.

"Can't stop?" I asked, bracing myself.

"*Levelors* aren't deploying," Mister Thomas admitted. "They were supposed to extend from the hull, and create a drag that would help us to slow down."

"Can you stop the engines?" I asked.

"No, not yet. That would cause us to lose too much altitude, too quickly," Mister Thomas said after thinking about it a minute.

"Can you reverse 'em?" I asked as the rock grew closer. Landing on that hard dirt were gonna be painful. "You want me to look at those *levelors*? See if I can get 'em unstuck? Or maybe you got an anchor you can drop?"

"An anchor! Of course! We could drop the second engine!" Mister Thomas proclaimed.

"Oh no we don't," I told him. "Tack again!" Heading straight into the wind wouldn't slow us: We'd flounder.

"Hang on!" Mister Thomas shouted as we come around, hard.

The carriage swung up high. Bags not tied down toppled to the other side of the cabin. I held on for dear life as we reached the top of the swing, then fell back with a jerk toward the other side.

I threw myself into the corner. The cabin was just attached with ropes, and it seemed easy enough to undo the cinches.

We were *not* gonna drop that second engine. That was just throwing out the baby with the bathwater. Who knew if we'd be able to fly out with the first engine running so hot?

But we could drop *ourselves* to act as a weight against the wind.

The cabin was only attached to the flying balloon by ropes, one in each corner cinched up with strong metal wheels.

I hit that first cinch with the palm of my hand, hard, unlocking the wheel that wound the rope attaching the cabin to the balloon. That side of the cabin fell with a sharp, stomach lurching drop.

"What are you doing?" Mister Thomas shouted as he tried to steer the lopsided load. He stepped onto a footstep under the dashboard: Seemed that was part of the balloon, not attached to the cabin.

"Giving us an anchor!" I told him as I attacked the cinch in the opposite corner.

"Brilliant!" Mister Thomas said. He came about again, slowing us down more.

The second cinch came off easier, and without as much of a drop.

Maybe we'd get out of this without too much damage.

The third cinch was more stubborn, and I bruised my hand slamming it. I didn't stop to find a wrench or something. Just hit it, hard.

With a squealing complaint it let go and we dropped.

I skidded toward that corner. Slammed into the rail and held on. Didn't topple over like a rag doll, because I was *damned* if I was gonna die that way, falling from the sky.

I clawed my way back up to the other side of the cabin and released the last cinch as Mister Thomas brought us around one last time.

The cabin slid level, about six feet under where Mister Thomas and the dashboard stood.

The airship slowed.

We sailed inches away from the big nose of the old miner and dropped further, going down into a green valley, hitting the grass with a heavy *thud*.

I held on and stayed to my feet, but just barely. The loose bags skidded across the floor. The airship stayed floating above me.

Mister Thomas looked down and gave me that twinkling smile of his. "See Gracie? We made it! Safe and sound."

I opened my mouth to give him a piece of my mind, then shut it again. Wouldn't do no good. Mister Thomas were just a boy at heart, with adventure on his mind. He thought he were invulnerable.

I knowed better.

It didn't take too long to get camp set up—two small canvas tents for sleeping and a lean-to over the existing fire pit for the kitchen. I wouldn't have told Mister Thomas, but it sure were handy having that automaton of his to unload stuff from the airship.

The hills here was bare of trees: Mister Thomas said it were due to the mining, using high-powered water hoses to wash away all the rock, then sluicing out the gold.

Made me kind of sad. These hills shoulda been filled with critters, birds and the like. But they was quiet. Bare rock looking bleached like bone.

Just beyond the flat part where we had camp was a great sucking hole in the side of the hill—that dang mine Mister Thomas had acquired.

I knowed there was still something fishy about it. Didn't like the look of it at all.

While I'd set up camp, Mister Thomas had gone "exploring," excited as a boy. I just hoped he'd be back by dark.

I'd just started water boiling for some tea when our neighbors came calling. I didn't like the look of them any more than they was happy to see us here.

I was glad I'd dressed sensible. Not in my saloon dress, or in a church dress, but a navy-blue bicycling suit with bloomers that let me move. Mama would have tsked, but they was practical.

They also let me carry my revolver more easily, tucked into my waistband at the small of my back. I kept the rifle nearby as well, always in reach.

"Howdy neighbor," said the bearded one, coming up the hill. He'd been gentlemanly, once, I woulda bet. But he'd gone to seed, his eyes wild, like those cowpokes who came into the bar after being too many months on the trail. His formerly fine suit was patched and streaked with dirt. He wore solid black boots and carried a rifle easy over one shoulder.

His partner weren't much better. He had the look of a hillsman, eyes wary, watching the wind. His smile gaped with more holes than teeth, and he just had white whiskers, not a proper beard. He wore typical miner clothes, shirt and vest and trousers, all black and torn up.

"Name's Earl," the bearded one stated, hand out as if in friendship.

"Hold on right there," I told him, reaching for my own rifle. "Earl? What kind of an introduction is that?" I asked, using my most snooty, town-folk tones.

I weren't no lady, and I doubted I could sound like one for long, but that type of introduction just weren't proper. Not for two strange men coming up to a woman all alone, out here in the middle of nowhere.

Even if I could handle a gun better than either of those two fools.

"Oh-ho! A lady! That's what we got here, Ben," Earl said to his companion.

"Some lady. Just a fancy man's doxie," Ben replied, his accent thick, staring at my legs. He'd come from someplace south of where I'd growed up.

"Excuse me," came the frosty tones of Mister Thomas from behind me. "But that's no way to talk to my wife."

The two started. They hadn't been expecting Mister Thomas. I hadn't even known he were in camp—thought he was still off exploring.

"No harm meant," Earl said, his rifle going back up over his shoulder. "Just saying hello to our new neighbors."

Ben squinted at my hands. "Shouldn't she have a ring or something?"

"Do I look like the type who would wear frivolous jewelry when there's work to be done?" I asked, steamed. I glanced over my shoulder at Mister Thomas, who nodded at me.

With my free hand, I jerked out the necklace I always wore, with the ring my twice-dead husband Andrew had given me. "But to satisfy your curiosity," I said, waving it at them.

I doubted they was close enough to see the gears engraved on it. But if they was, well, it would have been appropriate for Mister Thomas as well. Andrew had also been an inventor, though not as good as Mister Thomas. There'd been no love lost between Andrew and me, particularly not when he came back after I'd thought he'd been killed and tried to reclaim me.

"Our mistake, lady," Earl said, his tones more cultivated, as if he were finally remembering his manners. Then he turned to Mister Thomas. "We couldn't help but notice you used an airship to arrive."

"Yes, of my own design," Mister Thomas said. Then he added, still using his coldest voice, "We wouldn't dream of using roads that we didn't have the right to."

"We appreciate that, we do," Earl said. "Just be sure to stick to your property, then, and we'll have no troubles."

"We will," Mister Thomas assured him. "But if you'll excuse us, gentlemen. It was a long journey here."

"Of course, of course," Earl said, bowing his head and backing away.

I knew it woulda been more polite to offer them tea or something. But I weren't feeling no more neighborly than Mister Thomas. "Good day, gentlemen," I said, holding myself stiff.

They both nodded their heads and ambled away.

I knew we'd be seeing them again, probably sooner rather than later.

However, there weren't nothing for it.

I turned to Mister Thomas. "Your wife?" I asked him, one eyebrow raised.

"A necessary fiction. And I knew you wore your ring from Andrew," Mister Thomas said, meeting my eye straight on.

I hadn't expected that. I'd a thought he'd be embarrassed about claiming me as a wife. He'd never shown any interest in any woman, not ever.

"Is the tea ready?" Mister Thomas said, still holding me steady in his regard.

"In a minute," I told him turning away.

He weren't watching me with a yearning in his eyes. Or at least that's what I told myself, despite how I felt his gaze burning a hole in my back.

"Let me show you the mine," Mister Thomas insisted after we'd finished the tea.

I looked dubiously at that dark hole. It weren't right. I just knew it.

Still, it were better to know how bad it could be. "Fine," I said, putting up the rest of the dishes. "You think the camp's safe, with both of us gone?" I asked him. I didn't have to specify that I was talking about our new neighbours.

"Safe enough," Mister Thomas said. "Mac can give us a shout if something goes awry."

"Mac?" I asked, looking around.

The silver man automaton walked up and planted itself in front of the lean to, arms crossed over its chest like a guard.

It would never have occurred to me to name a machine that way.

And if Earl or Ben shot the machine, we'd hear that as well.

"All right," I said, dusting off my hands and following Mister Thomas up the hillside.

The dark cave breathed out cold on me. It smelled of wet rock and dirt, with maybe a hint of sulphur. The sound of water trickling, like a broken pipe, echoed loud in the skinny entrance.

Mister Thomas had already put up some of his fancy flickering lights, so I could see just how tall the entrance went: Up and up, like some kind of giant pine.

"This weren't manmade, was it?" I asked Mister Thomas as we walked along easily side by side. I'd been expecting having to bend in half once we got through the opening.

"The entrance? No. It was caused by the erosion of a limestone pocket in the granite," Mister Thomas told me.

I just nodded like I understood.

A few feet inside, around a hunk of rock, stood a skinny wooden table, right legs shorter than the left, making the top slant.

I shivered at the sight: It looked to me like an altar to something ungodly. Vials and glass jars I'd normally seen in Mister Thomas' laboratory were spread across it, bubbling pink and wretched green and burping purple, along with a burner and spigot.

"I was trying to find the alkahest," Mister Thomas hurriedly explained, drawing me forward.

The stench of his chemicals made my eyes water and sent more chills down my spine. "What's that?" I asked. It sounded foreign.

"It's a universal solvent, able to dissolve every other substance it comes in contact with," Mister Thomas told me.

I didn't snort him. I coulda whipped up a batch of Mama's special moonshine that woulda done that for him, even pitting any glass it was kept in.

"I failed in my search," Mister Thomas said, rushing to the other side of the table.

"I'm sorry," I told him. Should I offer to make him that moonshine?

"No, Gracie, it was extremely fortuitous," Mister Thomas assured me. "Instead of a universal solvent, I found one that merely dissolved the rock around gold. And it collects the gold together as well."

"So you'd only be dissolving the right parts, instead of destroying the hills around here," I said, nodding. That was real smart of him.

"Yes!" Mister Thomas uncovered a jar sitting to one side of the table. "And even this hard granite dissolves as easily as washing away soap scum."

In the centre of his hand lay a misshapen lump of gold, as big as a baby's fist. A second one, identical in size and shape, lay on the table.

"My goodness!" I said, coming forward. Was we really gonna be rich? Maybe I should have taken up his original offer.

"Here," Mister Thomas said, handing the gold to me.

It felt warm and heavy in my palm. "What's that?" I asked, rubbing my thumb across it.

Gold flaked away, leaving plain rock underneath.

"Damn it!" Mister Thomas said. He reached for a pair of goggles on the table, wrapping them around his head, making his eyes bug out. He gently held my hand and turned it, his palm warm against mine, his fingers stronger than I woulda given him credit for. "I think it collects together not just gold, but the pyrite, fool's gold, as well."

"Ah," I said. It was clear to me that Mister Thomas had been tricked into this mine, thinking it was full of real gold.

"Ah, indeed, Gracie old girl," Mister Thomas said with a sad smile. He kept ahold of my hand, like he didn't realize he was still touching me. "You should keep this one," he said softly. "Though I doubt you need any more reminders of my follies."

I was about to tell him that it was gonna be all right when several shots rang out from outside the cave.

Mister Thomas snatched back his hand as if it had been burned.

I took the lump of gold and dumped it down my shirt, hiding it in my bosom. "Bring that," I instructed Mister Thomas, pointing at the other lump, as I shouldered my rifle and led us out of the cave.

Earl was standing just outside, looking as pleased as those big game hunters who'd shot them a lion out in Africa.

Mac was unhurt.

But the airship balloon had folded in on itself and collapsed, looking like a heap of dirty linen.

"Sorry about that," Earl announced as we emerged. "I thought I'd seen a wild cat, up in the rocks, slinking down to enter the cave where you two were."

I looked over at Mister Thomas without lowering my rifle. He knew as well as I did that no matter how often we patched up the balloon, Earl or Ben would just shoot it up again.

Maybe waiting next time until we'd taken off. Damn fool was just lucky he hadn't ignited the balloon and himself in a ball of glory.

"So it looks as though we might be needing to buy passage on your road," Mister Thomas said. He looked casually at the lump of gold in his hand.

Earl's eyes grew as round as a Chinaman's. "I'm certain we can work out some kind of equitable deal," he said. "Like free passage for all the gold you've dug out since you've arrived here."

"What, this?" Mister Thomas said. "I'm not sure about that." Mister Thomas looked at me. "What do you say, Gracie?"

"Half-a-dozen trained mules, with empty packs, good maps, and food to last us a week," I instructed. "Then we'll hand over the gold."

"We could just take it," Earl said, stepping forward.

I put a bullet half an inch in front of his boot, then raised the rifle back up again to his face. "Not alive, you couldn't."

"You got yourself a hellcat there, don't you?" Earl asked, taking a step back.

"You have no idea what a treasure she is," Mister Thomas said, his voice warmer than I'd ever remembered hearing it before.

Hell, I almost believed him.

It didn't take long for the mules to arrive, with good packs. The maps were iffy, but Mister Thomas felt he could get us out. We was gonna have to abandon the airship, but we salvaged as much of the machinery as we could. Mac helped, tearing the wood apart easily in his mechanical hands.

Ben and Earl just sat there, watching. I don't think they'd ever seen a woman working beside a man before. But Mister Thomas treated me like an equal, capable of handling all the equipment on my own.

Which I mostly could. However, I also kept my rifle handy, in case our neighbours decided to get less friendly.

Mister Thomas broke all the vials in the cave, smashing them against the wall, almost as if he were angry. But his face never lost that small half smile of his, like this were all going according to plan.

We set out that day even though it was late, wanting to get to the next dale before the sunset. It would take us a week to get back to Stockton, sooner if we met up with the train.

I rode out of camp backwards, my rifle trained first on Earl, then on Ben. But they weren't paying us no mind, fondling the gold nugget that Mister Thomas had finally handed over to them.

"We can go back sometime," I told Mister Thomas as we finally ambled out of eyesight. "See if there's some real gold up there."

"I afraid we can't," Mister Thomas said. "That was the other need for the swiftness of an airship. I only acquired the mine for three weeks."

"I'm sorry," I told Mister Thomas. I knew he'd spent a lot of money on his equipment and getting us there. He were much more in the hole, now.

Which meant he'd start gambling again, which were never good.

"I'm fine, Gracie," Mister Thomas assured me. "I don't know what I would have done without you."

"You'd a managed," I told Mister Thomas. I didn't want him looking or sounding so sad. Or so friendly-like either.

"I would have had to," Mister Thomas said, turning resolutely forward. "It would have been the proper thing to do. And we must be proper. No matter how we feel, or what confounds us, or the trials we may face." He flicked his eyes at me, staring hard for a moment, then looked back ahead.

I may not have been able to read my letters, but I could sure tell what he meant. For all his talk about me saving him and us pretending for even an afternoon to be man and wife, we came from different classes.

It wouldn't be right for us to ever be more than employer and employee.

Mister Thomas navigated us to the train after only two days, which got us back into Stockton in three. When I was alone in my garret I finally took off my blouse and looked at the single nugget we'd gotten out of the hills.

Riding as it had, tight against my chest, had rubbed off the first coat of fool's gold, as well as the layer of darker rock around it, turning my skin black and shiny.

Underneath lay another nugget, much smaller. I didn't even need to taste it to know it were pure gold.

I sat on my bed in my small attic, holding it in the palm of my hand. I'd said I'd split seventy percent of the gold we found with Mister Thomas. It weren't fair for me to keep it all to myself.

And Mama had raised me to be mostly fair.

I knew what he'd say when I showed it to him: That I should keep it, maybe move out of my little garret. Get that land I'd been hankering for. Maybe move out of Stockton, start a farm, no longer be a barmaid.

As if I'd ever leave California without him.

I left it sitting on the table next to my bed all night, dreaming of things I'd never have.

Morning came, and I put those foolish dreams away, heading into the saloon just a little bit early to share the news with Mister Thomas, my employer, and maybe, my friend.

ABOUT THE AUTHOR

Leah Cutter currently lives in Seattle--the land of coffee and fog. However, she's also lived all over the world and held the requisite odd writer jobs, such as doing archeology in England, teaching English in Taiwan, and bartending in Thailand.

She writes fantasy set in exotic times and locations such as Tang dynasty China, WWII Budapest, rural Louisiana, and the Oregon coast.

Her short fiction includes literary, fantasy, mystery, science fiction, and horror, and has been published in magazines as well as anthologies and on the web.

Read more stories by Leah Cutter at www. KnottedRoadPress.com.

Follow her blog at www.LeahCutter.com.

ABOUT KNOTTED ROAD PRESS

Knotted Road Press fiction specializes in dynamic writing set in mysterious, exotic locations.

Knotted Road Press non-fiction publishes autobiographies, cookbooks, and how-to books with unique voices.

Knotted Road Press creates DRM-free ebooks as well as high-quality print books for readers around the world.

With authors in a variety of genres including literary, poetry, mystery, fantasy, and science fiction, Knotted Road Press has something for everyone.

Knotted Road Press
www.KnottedRoadPress.com